the BIG ROAD

the
BIG ROAD

by TOM E. CLARKE

LOTHROP, LEE & SHEPARD
NEW YORK

© 1965 by Tom E. Clarke
Library of Congress Catalog Card Number: 64–17042

Third printing, August, 1966

To Heavy, who inspired this book,
and to Jean, my wife, who made it possible.

the BIG ROAD

1

Raindrops trickled down the barrel of the .22 cradled in Vic Martin's arms; his clothes were drenched and his shoes squished in the mud. The yellow dog, standing close against his leg, was as wet as he.

They stood on a tree-lined bluff just back of the beach between Port Discovery and Sequim Bay on the northern rim of the Olympic Peninsula in the state of Washington. It was late in April 1933.

A chill wind sent gray combers crashing onto Dead Man's Spit, a hundred feet below, drove stinging rain into their faces, and then whistled off into the woods behind them.

Except for a narrow strip of calm water a mile offshore in the lee of Protection Island, everywhere the boy looked there were whitecaps on the sea. The black buoy marking the edge of the shoals westward of the island was almost obscured by mist and spindrift. It was good fishing out around that buoy, he knew, and one day soon when his boat was built he'd be out there jigging for cod and halibut, trolling for salmon, and hauling crab pots.

For two years Vic had dreamed of the sailboat he'd build. He'd seen her in a magazine, and sent a dime in for the plans. Now he was accumulating the things to build her with. The ribs and planking would be of driftwood he'd beachcombed, brought home and stored in a corner of the barn. The keel would be a big oak timber that had washed up from a wrecked schooner, and as soon as he figured out a way to get it home from the beach he could start building.

He'd squirreled away enough money to buy screws and nails and paint from the odd quarters he'd earned digging clams and picking berries. Some time this summer maybe he'd have her launched. And on a day like this he could just see himself—standing at the tiller, bundled up in yellow oilskins, sailing close-hauled beyond Protection Island. North of Protection were the San Juans. Beyond them was Canada, and beyond Canada, Alaska. Who knew how far he'd go?

A flash in the northwest caught Vic's eye. It was the beacon of the lighthouse on Dungeness Spit, eight miles away, winking out a warning to the mariners who passed by, inbound from the ocean, outbound from Puget Sound. There was a ship out there now, the gray ghost of a destroyer knifing through the darkening gloom of late afternoon. He watched longingly as the naval vessel went out of sight behind the island. He'd never been off the Olympic Peninsula.

And now that he had turned seventeen, he was old enough to join the Navy, if he wanted to.

Anything was better than being a farm boy on a stump ranch, he had decided, and the sea held a special attraction for him. Whenever he could he'd take time off from hunting the cows and fight his way through the tangled brush to the edge of the bluff, just so he could stand for a few minutes and look out at the water.

Vic snapped his fingers and the dog pricked up his ears. "That's all for today, Jack, let's go find the cows." They were a good three miles from home and would have to hurry to get back before dark. Vic ducked his lean frame and began working through the thicket. His shoulder bumped a bush and he was drenched again by the cold rain water that had accumulated on the leathery salal leaves.

He wished sometimes that those blasted cows would stray so far he'd never find them again! But with water on three sides and a railroad right-of-way fence on the fourth, there wasn't much chance of that. There were, however, a thousand gullies and ravines where cows could hide in these logged-off hills, and they knew them all.

Sometimes it seemed to Vic that his whole life was geared to the needs of the family cows. He got up at five o'clock in the morning to feed and milk them, then after cleaning the barn, he herded them to the north property line gate and turned them loose to graze along the logging roads that crisscrossed the rough, unsettled country beyond. Each evening when he got home from school, after he had the woodbox and water buckets filled, he had to go out looking for them, bring them in to feed and milk, then clean the barn again.

It wasn't so much that he disliked cows or farm-work. It was really his stepfather that got him down, and made him long to get away from his belittling attitude. Especially when he called him "Useless," as he did whenever Vic left a job undone, or did it in a way that was not up to his standard.

Vic had once complained bitterly to his mother. "Can't you make him stop calling me that?"

"Perhaps if you did less daydreaming and more work," she replied, "he wouldn't have reason to."

"He'd find some reason," Vic muttered. "Do you always have to take his side?"

But she had only wrinkled her brow in an unmistak-able sign of growing irritation and Vic knew he wasn't going to get any sympathy.

Well, when he had his boat built, things would be different. He could go sailing off on his own then, with no one to grouch at him and criticize everything he did. But at least he'd stuck it out longer than his older sister, Marie. She'd left home a couple of years ago, and now she was married.

Vic reached the skid road, deserted and unused since logging operations had shut down in 1930. The Depression had pinched off a demand for lumber and the logs from which it was cut, and now only an occasional wood thief, poacher or moonshiner used the roads.

The grass between the ruts had grown almost to his knees, and today it was undisturbed. Obviously the cows had not come this way. And what a day to hunt for them! The trees were threshing so in the wind he wouldn't be able to hear the cowbells until he was right on top of them.

When the weather was decent Vic didn't mind these jaunts. It was a chance to get away from the endless dull jobs that were part of turning forty acres of stumpland into a producing farm. He often saw deer, grouse or quail, and plenty of cottontails. That's why he had the .22 along. But on a windy day like this, he'd just wasted his energy carrying it. He couldn't tell his mother that though. When he'd left the house she'd said, "We're out of meat again, Victor. Try and get some today."

And he'd answered, "There won't be anything out in this wind, Mom. I'll go to the beach and get a mess of clams instead. There's a low tide this afternoon."

"I'm tired of clams."

"Let's eat that old Plymouth Rock then. She doesn't lay any more."

"Why, Fanny is the best brood hen we have! Try to get something, even if it's only a rabbit."

Vic said he'd try. He was as hungry for meat as anyone.

They raised plenty of vegetables on the place, the cows produced all the milk and butter they could use, and they had lots of eggs from the flock of Rhode Island Red chickens. It was meat that was always scarce. You could fill up on potatoes for a while, but without meat you soon got a gnawing in your stomach. Especially when you were six-foot-two and weighed only a hundred-twenty. So he'd brought his gun along.

During a brief lull in the wind he stood still, hoping to hear the tinkle of a cowbell. But the dull roar of the surf behind him drowned out all other sounds. "Come on, Jack," he said, "let's go around this way. Maybe Dan Jones has seen them."

He turned west and started down the skid road toward Dan Jones's logging camp. Several years ago a forest fire had burned, leaving only a stand of dead trees behind. A rank growth of willow and alder had sprung up since the fire. If any deer were out today that's where they'd be, browsing on the saplings in the shelter of the blackened snags.

He hadn't gone far when up ahead the dog stopped and pointed off into the burn. Jack was a cross between a collie mother and a German shepherd father, and he was a good hunter. Tensed, he stood with ears erect, one front paw uplifted, tail stiff and quivering.

Vic hurried forward, bent low and treading lightly. "What is it, boy?" he whispered.

Jack growled softly, holding his stance. Vic got directly behind the dog, sighted down his back and over his nose. At first he saw nothing but the shadows among the ghostly trees. Then there was a movement and he made out a patch of tawny hair. It looked like a deer, but he had to be dead sure before he fired. And with a .22 you had to know exactly where you were aiming or all you'd do was wound the animal, leaving it to go off some place to die in misery.

With the rain dripping off his hat brim and trickling icily down his neck, Vic settled down to watch. He didn't have long to wait.

Before he even saw it move, the deer was half out in the open, eyes inquisitive, ears flicking nervously. She turned her head away to nibble at a willow, and Vic whipped the gun to his shoulder, cocking it silently. The next time she looked his way he'd pull the trigger. He wanted to put the shot squarely between the eyes, to make the killing swift and sure.

The deer took a step forward and came farther out into the open, giving him a full view of her body. It was deep and distended. She was soon to have a fawn. No wonder she was out feeding in the wind.

Vic took the gun from his shoulder and lowered the hammer. When he reached back to turn his collar up, the deer, startled, sprang out of sight into the thicket. "All right, Jack," Vic said, "it's time we left, too." He plodded on down the logging road. The dog followed, looking back now and again in the direction the doe had gone. Poor Jack, it had been a long time since he'd had a bone to gnaw on.

But Vic felt relieved. Killing a rabbit or a grouse out of season was one thing, but a mother deer was something else. It wasn't right and he knew it. Of course, no one worried too much about being caught these

13

days. The game wardens were only paid a share of the fines they collected, and since no one had any money anyway, the wardens stayed pretty much out of the woods except to make an occasional arrest to show they were on the job.

A little way farther on, Vic came to the logging camp, a dreary group of tar paper covered buildings set haphazardly in a clearing among the head-high stumps. He walked past an open shed housing a partly dismantled tractor and two ancient trucks. Empty oil drums and coils of rusted cable were strewn about nearby. Beyond the shed was the bunkhouse and next to it the cookshack with a triangle dangling in the wind outside the door. Dan Jones lived in the cookshack so he could keep an eye on things during the shutdown. He didn't seem to be at home today, though. No smoke was coming from the stovepipe and his car was missing from its parking place.

Vic reached the edge of the clearing and saw a great patch of morels sprinkled through the scrubby grass. His mother was especially fond of these spongelike mushrooms. They were the first to appear in the springtime and were very good eating. There were dozens of them, enough to take the place of meat for two meals at least. There would be plenty of butter to cook them in—with six cows they were always sure of that. Vic got a wooden box from the trash heap outside the cookshack, and started picking them. He had just about finished when Dan Jones's old black sedan came chugging around the bend. Vic stood up and waved, and the Ford came to a shuddering stop beside him. "You had a bunch of morels here, Mr. Jones. I hope you don't mind my picking them."

"First come, first served."

"Want some?"

"No, thanks. I'm scared to eat the things."

"You don't know what you're missing."

"I have to pick up some tar paper, then I'll be heading back your way, Vic. Climb in and I'll give you a ride home."

"Thanks, but I've got to round up the cows, Mr. Jones."

"They were standing in the barnyard when I drove through your place a little while ago. Must have come back on their own on account of the rain. Hop in."

Vic crawled in next to Mr. Jones. Jack jumped into the back seat, and they lurched up the rutted road to the bunkhouse.

A dozen rolls of tar paper stood upended in a corner of the musty-smelling building.

"We'll only need about four, I guess," Mr. Jones said. He picked up two rolls and started for the door.

Vic picked up the others. "What's it for?" he asked.

"Smith's roof caught fire this morning. We're going to try to patch it up so they'll have a place to stay tonight." He piled the rolls on the floor in the back of the car and got in.

The road leading away from camp was crooked,

winding in and out among the stumps and standing timber. On the downgrades Mr. Jones hung grimly onto the wheel and Vic clutched at his box of mushrooms while they coasted wildly down one slope to build up enough momentum to get the old sedan up the next.

Then they were out of the trees, rolling across a half-cleared field toward a cluster of farm buildings, and Vic was home. It was still light enough to see the cows standing beside the barn, and the chicken coop and house beyond. Smoke was blowing from the chimney and yellow lamplight glowed from the windows.

The car stopped by the barn and Vic got out. "Thanks a lot, Mr. Jones. When I'm done with the milking I'll come over to Smith's and lend a hand."

Vic went into the barn and leaned the .22 in a corner. He set the mushrooms down on the work bench and glanced toward the far wall where his boat materials had been stored. Then, angrily, he ran to the house, slamming the door behind him. He burst into the kitchen, almost bowling over Fred, his ten-year-old half brother.

"Who took my boat lumber?"

His mother looked up from stirring a bowl of cornbread batter. "You mean those old boards out in the barn?"

"They aren't just old boards! Where are they?"

Nancy, his half sister who was nine, was setting the table. "The Smiths' roof burned off this morning," she volunteered, butting in as usual. "Mom gave them your boards to fix it."

"But, Mom, those were to build my boat with!"

"You're being selfish, Victor. The Smiths need a roof more than you need a boat. And besides, your father wants that space in the barn," she said as he continued to sulk. "Go get your milking done."

"Don't call him *my* father!" Vic shouted.

The tired look on his mother's thin face deepened and she reminded him again, as she had done so often, how good his stepfather had been to him and Marie. But that had just been when they were little. After Fred and Nancy were born Vic and Marie had felt left out. Vic had wanted to run off plenty of times, but he'd always hung around hoping things might change. He knew his mother really did need him. He knew she loved him, too, but why couldn't she show it?

Vic took the tin basin from its nail by the door and slammed it down on the wash stand. He filled it with cold water from the bucket, washed his face and hands, then lighted a lantern. As he was going out the door, his mother said, "Did you get any game?"

"No, but I found some morels. They're in the barn."

"Freddie, you go with Vic and bring them in. We'll have some for supper."

The lantern light was shining on the empty space in the barn where his lumber had been. Vic looked at it a moment then turned angrily to his half brother.

"Say, Fred, isn't it about time you learned to milk?"

"Why should I? That's your job." The boy picked up the box of mushrooms and ran to the house.

"Well, you'd better start learning!" Vic called after him. To himself, he added, "Because I won't be here in the morning to do it."

And this time he meant it.

2

Vic closed the gate quietly behind him, slung a partly filled gunny sack over his shoulder, and walked up the county road. He was off to join the Navy.

During the night the rain had stopped and the wind had died away. The moon came out from behind the clouds, outlining his shadow as he walked along. There was a dusting of new snow upon the Olympics that formed a barrier across the southern sky. Spring had come to the lowlands but winter was still on the mountaintops. Even here the air was chilly and Vic had to walk briskly to keep warm. Directly to the east, above the distant Cascade Mountains, the sky was brightening. In another hour the sun would rise and the day was going to be a good one.

He'd had trouble getting to sleep last night and, awakening earlier than usual, had snuggled under the warmth of the heap of old coats and quilts that covered his cot. Maybe leaving home wasn't such a good idea after all. He was still undecided when the alarm clock rang. He turned it off and burrowed deeper into the bedding. Maybe he should stick it out a while longer. He had just about convinced himself to give it one more try when there was a hard rapping on the opposite wall and his stepdad's voice said sharply, "Get a move on out there, Useless!"

That had done it.

He'd jumped out of bed in the darkness and got hurriedly into his cold clothes. Following his usual routine so as not to arouse anyone's suspicions, he'd lighted the lantern and gone around to the kitchen, built the fire in the cookstove and put on the coffee pot. Then he'd washed and left the house. But instead of going to the barn he'd set the lantern and milk buckets down on the well, got the gunny sack in which he'd packed his belongings the night before, and cut across the field to the road. When the rest of them got up they were in for a surprise.

His mother would fix breakfast, and when he didn't come back from milking she'd step out onto the back porch to call him. She'd see the lantern and the buckets sitting on the well and would look into his lean-to and find the note he'd left telling her where he'd gone. By the time she'd read it he would be halfway to Port Ludlow and the ferry that would take him to Seattle.

There was a rustle in the roadside bushes and Vic saw a shadow skulking there. "All right, Jack, I see you." He snapped his fingers and the dog came bounding out, wagging his tail. Vic bent and patted him.

"You can't go with me today, boy." The dog's ears fell, his tail drooped. "Go home now." Jack took a step or two away, and looked back expectantly. "Go on, beat it!"

The dog ran back as far as the gate. He was standing there watching as Vic turned and began walking fast, not daring to look back again.

He could still hear the sound of cowbells behind the barn, and from the chicken coop there came the defiant crow of Struttin' Sam. Moments later, from the distance, there echoed an answer from a neighbor's rooster.

It was almost a mile to the highway and he was going to have to hurry to catch a ride on the milk truck. It was due by at half past four and it must be four-fifteen already. He went up and over a low hill, and the early morning farmyard sounds were shut out behind him.

Ahead, at the low place just this side of the railroad crossing he could see water running across the road. The culvert must have got plugged again. In the flooded ditch to the right a green-headed mallard drake and his somber-feathered mate were swimming. They lifted from the water at his approach, climbed steeply, and vanished over the treetops, wind whistling in their beating pinions. What a pair of beauties they were!

As he neared the shallow stream of water flowing across the roadway, Vic made a running jump. One foot tangled with the other and he splashed a good two feet from the far side. Wading out, he went on to the crossing and sat down on a railroad track, took off his shoes, emptied them and squeezed the water out of his socks. They were the only socks and shoes he had. At least three sizes too large, they'd turned up in a sackful of hand-me-downs that one of the county commissioners had brought out at Christmas time. Everything he had, had come out of a sack like that and nothing ever fitted.

Last year he could have had a good outfit of clothes to start school in. He'd earned twenty-eight dollars in a week of scorching, twelve-hour August days fighting a big forest fire on top of Blyn Mountain. Someone had set the fire, it was rumored, so people could have work.

When Vic's paycheck came, Dad said, "Now I can get those new front tires for the Model-T."

"But that's *my* money!"

"Well, what if it is. It's time you started paying a little board around here," his stepfather told him. "If you don't want to hand over that check you can head off up that road—any time. It's entirely up to you."

Vic would have left then and there, but his mother had taken him aside and pleaded with him. "Please, Vic, let him have it. Anything to keep peace in the family. Please, for my sake."

So, for her sake, he'd given in and, as usual, the money had been lost in a poker game in the back room of the pool hall down at Blyn. No tires for the truck, no shoes for the kids and no new clothes for Vic. Mom had added another strip of denim to the bottoms of his overalls and lengthened his shirt sleeves another couple of inches. And then they wondered why a guy didn't particularly want to go to school when most of the other fellows in the class were wearing clothes that fit them, and some even had the latest in yellow cords and brown suede jackets with knit cuffs and collars.

No, sir, it wasn't just the cows and the woodpile and the boat lumber that had sent him off up the road. A guy could take just so much and nothing more.

Vic reached the highway and crossed over to the milk stand on the other side. He tapped one of the ten-gallon cans sitting there. It was full. Good, the truck hadn't come yet. He put his sack on the stand and listened. In the distance he could hear McVicar's dog barking. Robins were twittering in the nearby trees and a hungry calf was bawling out beyond them. Then to the west he heard the rumble of a heavy engine as the milk truck started, gained speed, and stopped again. It was making pickups at the farms down in Michigan Settlement and would take ten more minutes to get here. Vic fidgeted. He was anxious to be on his way.

He took out the money he'd saved toward the building of his boat. He counted it again. There wasn't much, but enough to get him to Seattle and buy food until he enlisted.

He looked back down the county line road he'd just

come along. He could see the roof of his own house over the treetops in the valley. A wisp of smoke was rising straight up from the chimney. Somebody had better get up soon and put another stick of wood in the stove or they'd have to build the fire again. But that wasn't his worry any more. He turned his head and reached in his pocket for his mouth organ. He played a few bars of "Red River Valley" and then stopped to listen for the milk truck.

He could hear it starting up the grade, a quarter mile away. Then its deep throbbing was drowned out by a high-pitched whine. It sounded like a fast-moving Model-A. The vehicle hardly slowed for the hill and as it popped over the crest Vic recognized the flatbed truck belonging to Mr. Frank, a grocer in Sequim, where he went to high school. He grabbed his sack and began to wave. The truck came to a skidding stop in the gravel on the shoulder of the highway and Mr. Frank reached over, unlatched the door and pushed it open. "Hello, Vic," he said. "Where you headed so early?"

"Seattle!"

"That's where I'm going. Hop in."

Vic tossed his sack over the side racks onto the back of the truck, and jumped into the cab.

"We're going to have to roll to catch that first boat," Mr. Frank said, working the gears and bringing the truck up to full speed. They broke out of the woods and passed the Gardiner schoolhouse. Vic caught a glimpse of the yellow school bus sitting in the shed behind it. At seven-thirty it would be on its way to Sequim. Well, it needn't stop at the county line this morning. And Mr. Edwards, the principal, wasn't going to like it at all. Vic had tried to drop out once before but Mr. Edwards had talked him out of it. "You've got too much to lose, Vic. This Depression isn't going to last forever and when things get rolling again you're one of the boys who some day will be in the driver's seat. But not if you don't have an education."

Beyond the schoolhouse, fields and farmhouses spread out before them. Sloping down from the highway to the blue waters of Discovery Bay were the orchards and berry fields owned by Mr. Gardiner. His dad worked here regularly and sometimes on weekends and vacations Vic helped out, too. But everything both of them made was applied to the grocery bill at Mr. Gardiner's store. They never got any cash, just worked to pay off the grocery bill.

As the truck started down the long hill beyond the school the engine roar diminished and the driver yelled over the whistling of the wind. "What are you going to Seattle for?"

"To join the Navy."

"What about school? Aren't you going to finish?"

"No more school for me."

Vic didn't much like studying, and he never had time after school to visit any of the kids his age who lived nearby. Not that that mattered, either, since his only really close friend had moved to Canada with his family last year.

Mr. Frank shook his head but said nothing.

Miles later they came around a bend and into Port Ludlow. The sun was just breaking over the trees across the channel as they rolled down the hill and came to a stop on the ferry dock behind several cars and trucks.

"Looks like we just made it," Mr. Frank said.

The ferry, with fresh white paint gleaming in the early morning sunlight, was creeping into the slip. Deckhands with hawsers stepped from deck to slip and made them fast; a ramp was dropped and the vehicles on board drove off and rumbled over the loose planks of the dock. The line of cars waiting to go aboard began to move and Mr. Frank pulled his truck into line.

As they neared the ticket-taker, Vic reached for his pocket. "How much does it cost?"

"Never mind," Mr. Frank said. "I'll get it. I don't mind helping someone who's trying to help himself."

"Thanks, Mr. Frank." Vic flashed him a smile.

When the brakes were set and the wheels blocked, the grocer asked, "How about breakfast?"

"I've had a little something."

"If you're like my boys you can always eat. Let's go up topside and have a bite."

"Well, I'll . . . I'll go have some coffee with you."

They went up the steep stairway to the passenger deck and into the restaurant amidships. They stood at the counter and the aroma of freshly brewed coffee, ham and eggs, and pancakes made Vic's mouth water. Tacked on the wall in front of them was a sign that said, "Please Pay When Served." Vic was reading it when a woman in a white apron came out of the small kitchen. "Hi!" She smiled at Mr. Frank. "Kind of early today, aren't you?"

"Got to be in Seattle by nine, Gert."

"What'll you have?"

"Pancakes, sausage and coffee to start."

The waitress filled a cup and set it down on the counter. She turned to Vic. "Same for you?"

He eyed the menu on the wall. "Uh . . . just the coffee, thanks. How much?"

"Five."

He took out a nickel and laid it down. Mr. Frank reached over and slid the coin back to him. "Give him the same as I'm having, Gert, plus a couple of eggs."

Vic started to protest.

"You're not getting it for nothing," Mr. Frank interrupted. "By the time we get the truck loaded at the grocery warehouse you're going to wish you'd had twice that much."

Vic grinned, and a moment later the ferry's sharp whistle made him jump. The bells jangled below, the engine started, and with a trembling of decks and tinkling of glass and silverware the ferry left the dock.

Through a window in the stern Vic could see a line of idle workers fishing along the dock and the receding smokestack of the silent lumber mill. Then the craggy peaks of the Olympics appeared above the timber at the end of Port Ludlow Bay. He was on his way at last!

3

"Let's go out and enjoy some of that sunshine," Mr. Frank said when they'd had their second cups of coffee. "We may not have it for too long." He pointed toward the line of clouds that was starting to creep in from the north.

They went out on the open deck. The water between them and the shore line was clear and green— here and there a duck bobbed on a swell or rode on a piece of driftwood. Gulls soared in the vessel's wake, swooping now and then to snatch and quarrel over scraps the cook threw overboard. A plank floated by, knot-free fir and perfect for a boat. Vic watched it pass astern.

"I never get tired of this trip," Mr. Frank said after a time.

"It's great!" Vic took a deep breath. This was his first boat ride.

A small fishing boat went by, outbound toward the ocean. They watched it toss about in the swell of the ferry. "What'll you do if you can't get in the Navy, Vic?"

"I don't know. I hadn't thought about that."

"Have to pass a pretty stiff physical to get in, you know."

"I'm as healthy as the next guy, Mr. Frank." The question had taken Vic by surprise.

"Still, there's a good chance they won't take you, underweight like you are. Then what?"

"I'll find something to do. I know how to work."

They passed a red buoy nodding in the tide rips, and Puget Sound opened up to the right and Mount Rainier appeared. The calm water reflected the white image of the solitary mountain. Vic had never seen it so close before and was surprised how much bigger it looked. It seemed to half fill the southeastern sky.

"There's the big town now," Mr. Frank said, nodding toward the buildings beginning to emerge in the smoky haze that hung over the land between the Sound and the stately mountain. The city itself was almost hidden.

"Some fifty thousand men are looking for work there, and most of them with hungry kids to feed. Competition's going to be tough." After some moments of silence he continued. "Why don't you ride around with me today and give me a hand, Vic, and I'll drop you off at home this afternoon? At least you'll have had the trip."

Vic didn't answer. He sat watching the details on shore take form—docks and smokestacks, oil tanks and buildings. Finally he shook his head. "I've milked my last cow, Mr. Frank."

"Oh, come on now, Vic, finish school. Even if you do get in the Navy, without a high school diploma you'll never be anything but another sailor. You've got to use your head to get ahead. I know you've had a rough time of it, but I'd hate to see you go off the deep end now."

"Thanks, Mr. Frank, but I'm not going back and that's that."

Nothing more was said. They neared the dock. It was lined with shabby-looking men sitting with bait cans and fishing lines, just like the ones they had seen on the other side.

Bells clanged below, the engine stopped, and the ferry drifted into the slip. "Let's go." Mr. Frank motioned and led the way downstairs to the vehicle deck where they got into the truck.

"Is this Seattle?" Vic asked.

"No, Edmonds. Seattle's still twenty miles from here."

The bells in the engine room clanged again. Churning water boiled past the hull, and they were docked. Beyond the pier end, parallel to the shore line, were the railroad tracks. A red light began flashing and a gong was dinging insistently as Mr. Frank drove off the ramp and stopped before the barricade that was lowered.

A warning whistle—two longs, a short, and a final drawn-out shriek—was still sounding as the locomotive came pounding from behind the corner of a sawmill. Smoke streamed from its stack and white steam trailed from the screaming whistle as the big black road engine thundered over the crossing. It was at least twice as long and half again as high as the little teakettle that hauled the weekly freight back home. It passed in an instant, whistling for the next crossing. And then came the long string of cars—boxcars, flatcars, gondolas, and tank cars—rattling and lurching and swaying and thumping. They came in all colors and sizes, and they bore the names of many of the nation's best known railroads—Sante Fe and Burlington; Frisco Line; the New York Central; B. & O.; the Erie; the Pennsylvania; the Chicago, Milwaukee, St. Paul & Pacific Railroad and many others.

Wherever they were from and wherever they were going, most of the cars had one thing in common: they all had people riding on them. They stood in the open doors of the boxcars or sat on the tops; they clung to the ladders on the sides of the tanks or crouched on the empty flatcars. There were white, black, red and yellow men; old men, young men, women and children. Occasionally one would wave and smile, and Vic waved back. There was a flash of red when the caboose cleared the crossing. Then the light stopped blinking, the gong stopped ringing, and the barricade was raised.

"Were all those people bums?" Vic asked as they moved across the tracks.

"I don't know," Mr. Frank said. "But every freight you see has a couple hundred on it."

"Where are they going?"

"I guess they just ride from place to place."

"How do they make a living?"

Mr. Frank shrugged. "They don't. That's why they're on the move." He pulled up at a stop sign, then turned right. "But I didn't see a fat man among them, did you?"

Vic shook his head.

They passed through the outskirts of the town and Mr. Frank speeded up for a run at the long hill ahead. When they reached the top, the engine roar finally died down a bit. "That train back there," Mr. Frank said, "will give you an idea of what you're going to be up against."

Vic didn't answer.

Half an hour later they were in Seattle. " 'The Queen City,' they call it," Mr. Frank said. The buildings weren't quite as tall as Vic had expected, and there weren't very many people on the streets yet. But the clattering streetcars fascinated him.

Mr. Frank drove to a wholesale grocery warehouse and took on half a load of canned goods. From there they went to a packing plant near the airport and put on meats. The last stop was at the platform of a bakery where the loading was completed. The sun was gone, the sky had completely clouded over, and a wind had sprung up. They just managed to tie down the canvas tarpaulin that covered the load before the cloudburst began.

"We're in for a good one," the grocer yelled and waved Vic into the truck. They drove away from the bakery and headed back toward the center of town.

"The recruiting office is probably in the Federal Office Building up there ahead of us, Vic. Are you still going to give it a try?"

"You bet. You can let me out at the light."

Mr. Frank pulled to the curb across the street from a brick building at the corner of First Avenue and Marion Street. On the sidewalk in front of the entranceway three large colorful signs beckoned: "Join the Army!" "Join the Navy! See the World!" "Be a Marine!"

"Well, this looks like the place all right." Vic smiled and reached for the handle of the door.

"I'll wait while you go in and talk to them. If it doesn't work out you come on back with me."

"Thanks, Mr. Frank, but you don't need to wait."

"You've really got your mind made up, haven't you?"

Vic nodded and shook the grocer's hand.

"Well, lots of luck." Mr. Frank reached into his overalls and took out a silver dollar. "Here, Vic. For your help."

"You've more than paid me already."

"Here, catch!" He flipped the dollar through the air. "Pay me back when you have a payday."

Vic caught the coin. The grocer waved and the truck drove away.

"So long and thanks for everything, Mr. Frank!"

The gutters were running full and the wind-blown rain funneling down First Avenue soaked him before he could get across the street and into the Federal Building.

Vic walked down the empty corridor, his hobnails echoing on the stone floor. He hesitated a moment before opening the door with "U. S. Navy Recruiting Service" lettered on it. When he did, a gray-haired man with a weather-beaten face looked up from a desk.

"Morning. What can I do for you?"

"I . . . I want to join the Navy."

The man got up and came over to the counter. He was wearing a blue uniform with brass buttons and gold insignia on his sleeve.

"And we'd like to have you."

"Swell." Vic's eyes lit up.

"Trouble is we're not taking any enlistments right now. They didn't give us enough money at the last session of Congress."

"How come you've got those signs out front, then?" Vic couldn't keep the disappointment out of his voice.

"Oh, we're still taking applications." He slid some papers in front of Vic. "Take these home and fill them out and mail them back. When enlistments open up again we'll notify you."

"Thanks." Vic folded the forms and put them in his pocket.

At the other recruiting offices in the building, Vic got the same answer. The Army, the Marine Corps, and the Coast Guard enlistments were all closed. Someone in the Coast Guard office said, "Why don't you try the Civilian Conservation Corps? They're taking men now for six months' enlistments."

"What's that?"

"The Government is opening up forest camps to fight fires and they're paying thirty dollars a month plus room and board and clothes."

"Are they in this building, too?"

"No, they're taking applications at the welfare board uptown in the Continental Building."

"Where's that?"

The man jotted down an address on a piece of paper and handed it to Vic. "Just go straight up First Avenue to Stewart Street, then east to Fourth Avenue. You can't miss it."

"Thanks a lot."

The wind was still blowing when Vic left the building but the rain had settled down to a light drizzle. He saw a big orange-colored streetcar coming his way and impulsively, when it stopped, he got on and put a dime in the fare box. He was a little disappointed however, when, before he was barely settled on one of the varnished seats, the conductor called, "Stewart Street!" He had expected a longer trip but at least he'd ridden on a streetcar.

Despite the weather there were a lot of people on the streets, hurrying from store to store with packages and shopping bags in their hands. Vic wondered where everyone got the money to buy so many things. A blue dress on a mannequin in a window caught his eye and he stopped to look at it. $4.98. Mom would look nice in that.

He hurried on up the street wondering now how Fred had made out with the cows this morning. There was no use kidding himself about it, though; his mother would be the one who'd end up doing the milking and barn-cleaning. But, he told himself, he'd soon be earning money. Thirty dollars a month with room and board and clothes. He could send something home every payday, and she could have a lot of things she'd never had before.

He reached the address he'd been given. A line of young men stood quietly under a marquee waiting their turn to go in. "Is this where you join the Conservation Corps?" he asked one of them.

"This is it."

Vic went to the end of the line and other men came along and fell in behind him. Before he'd got halfway to the door there were about a hundred more men waiting, and half a dozen Army trucks parked at the curb with soldiers at the wheels. Every once in a while a group of men would troop noisily out of the building, smile broadly, pile into a truck and be driven away. "I made it, Joe!" one called to an acquaintance in line. "See you at Fort Lawton!"

"He won't be seeing *me* at Fort Lawton," the fellow in front of Vic muttered.

"Where's Fort Lawton?" Vic asked him.

"Out on Magnolia, just this side of the canal."

"Oh." He didn't know any more than he had before. Others came out alone and hurried away with downcast eyes, disappointment reflected on their faces. It was apparent they weren't taking everybody. More to himself than to anybody else Vic said, "I hope they don't turn me down."

The fellow in front of him looked around. "Well, I hope they *do* turn me down." He was about twenty-one, and wore long sideburns and a pencil-line "cooky-duster" mustache. His black hair, full at the sides and long behind, was plastered down with slickum. There were bright red triangles set into the legs of his dungarees to make them bell-bottomed. Vic's stepdad would have called him a sheik.

"Why are you here, then, if you don't want to join?"

"One of the old gals from the welfare board told my folks if I didn't come down and try to get in the 3-C they'd cut off my allowance." He took a half-smoked cigarette from a crumpled package, put it into a long holder and lighted it. "Don't worry, by the time I get done talkin' they won't touch me with a ten-foot pole."

"What's wrong with joining?"

"Are you crazy? You have to send $25 of your pay home every month." The fellow drew deeply on his cigarette holder. "Why should I go out in the woods and work? Nobody's going to let me starve." He nodded toward Vic's sack. "Whatcha got in the bag?"

"Oh, just my things."

"What kinda things?"

"Shirt, overalls, towel, and some soap and stuff."

"You look like a farmer. Where you from?"

"Over on the Peninsula."

"I thought so."

At noon the line stopped moving while the workers inside went to lunch. Vic was getting hungry himself, but he didn't want to lose his place. There were at least two hundred men and boys behind him now, standing quietly with their backs to the wind, their collars turned up. There was little talk.

A gaunt young woman wearing shabby clothes came down the line, handing out sheets of paper. "Don't join, boys," Vic heard her say. "The CCC is a trap by the capitalist Government!" She shoved one into Vic's hand. "Go home, Slim. Protest this scheme of the capitalist butchers. Go home. Don't join!" Vic glanced down at the mimeographed paper.

PROTEST! PROTEST! PROTEST!
DON'T JOIN THE CCC!

Don't be taken in by the dirty capitalists' lies!
Come to a mass meeting at First and Main this
afternoon and hear THE TRUTH about how the
Government is going to use you to put down the
REVOLUTION OF THE PROLETARIAT!
Workers, don't turn on your Comrades!

FREE COFFEE! FREE COFFEE!
FREE COFFEE!

Central Communist Party
of the State of Washington.

The ink was still wet and the paper smudged Vic's
fingers.

"Well," the sideburned fellow in front said, after
reading the paper, "I think it makes sense."

"Oh, bush-wah!" another said. "I don't care what
the Government does with me as long as they give me
a job."

"The communists don't want us to have jobs,"
someone else said. "The hungrier we get, the better
their spiel will sound."

Vic tossed away the sheet. The wind whipped it
into a gutter and carried it into the grating of a storm
drain.

At one o'clock the line began to inch forward again,
but it was another hour before Vic got out of the
drizzle and into the building. It was warm inside and
smelled of damp clothing and men's bodies. A dozen
male clerks sat at typewriters asking questions and
filling out forms.

At the far end of a large hall doctors were tapping
chests, listening to hearts, and examining teeth and
throats. A soldier was weighing and measuring the
men. Vic felt better when he saw that a lot of the
men being accepted were almost as thin as he was.

He listened as the fellow in front of him was being questioned. He gave his name, address, and place of birth. When asked his age he said "Seventeen."

Vic could have sworn he was at least four or five years older.

The clerk looked up. "Did you say seventeen?"

"That's what I said—seventeen."

"What year were you born?"

"I, uh . . ." the fellow hesitated. "Nineteen, uh . . . 1917, I guess."

The clerk was skeptical. "Are you sure it was 1917?"

"That's what I said, didn't I?"

"As far as I'm concerned you could pass for twenty-one."

"I'm seventeen!"

"Okay." The clerk typed some lines on the form and flipped it out of the machine. "You have to be eighteen, so I guess that disqualifies you."

"Can you give me something to prove to the welfare board I couldn't get into the 3-C?"

"We'll notify them."

"Thanks." The fellow winked at Vic as he turned and left the building.

Well, Vic thought, I guess that lets me out, too. But I'll give it a try. He stepped up and took his place in front of the desk. "Your name, please?" the clerk said.

"Vic—Victor Martin."

"Where do you live?"

"Gardiner, Washington."

"Gardiner? Where's that?"

"Over on the Olympic Peninsula."

"Oh, then it isn't in King County?"

"No, it's in Jefferson but our place is just over the line in Clallam County."

The clerk shook his head. "Sorry, Martin. We're only taking men whose homes are in King County."

"You mean I can't join?"

"Not here. You'll have to apply through your welfare board in Port Angeles." He took the unfinished form out of the typewriter and dropped it into the wastebasket. "Good luck," he said. "Next man, please."

4

Vic left the building. From what he'd heard while standing in line, he knew they wouldn't take him into the Civilian Conservation Corps in Port Angeles, either. You weren't eligible to join unless your family was on relief, and thank goodness his wasn't.

His stepdad took a lot of pride in never having gone to the welfare board, and that was *one* thing Vic had to admire him for. He hadn't objected to accepting old clothes and Christmas baskets from the politicians. But not relief. No, sir. He wouldn't have any of it. He said he'd rather starve.

Vic stepped into the doorway of an unoccupied store building to get out of the rain while he took stock of things. He counted his money again—two dollar bills, a silver dollar, four dimes, a nickel, and some pennies. He tucked one of the paper dollars into his shirt pocket and buttoned down the flap. That was enough to buy a ferry ticket, and if he hadn't found a job by the time his money was gone, maybe he'd think about going back to the Peninsula. The problem right now was that he was hungry. He wondered where he could get the most for what he had to spend.

Up the street, just a little way ahead, he saw the fellow who'd been in front of him in the CCC line. "Hi! I thought you'd gone home," Vic called.

"Ain't been able to raise the carfare yet."

"Where do you live?"

"About a mile from here."

Only a mile! Fred and Nancy walked better than four miles a day just getting back and forth to school. Let him walk, Vic thought.

"Well," the fellow said, "I guess I'd better start hoofin' it if I want to get any supper."

"Do you know a good place to eat where the prices aren't too high?" Vic asked.

The fellow's eyes brightened. "You got some money on you?"

"A little bit."

"I know just the place." He took Vic by the arm.

"Just tell me where it is. I can find it all right."

"Oh, you could never find this place by yourself. I'll come along and show you how to get there." He steered Vic across the intersection against the traffic light and they went down the street toward the bay. "You're gonna like this place, Speed," he said. "They give you all you can eat for four bits." He bent and scooped up a cigarette butt lying in a doorway, stopped and put it into his holder and lighted it. "The trouble with these blasted rainy days," he said as they went on, "is it makes it hard to find any decent smokes. Once a snipe gets wet it's ruined." He held the yellowed holder out to Vic. "Want a puff?"

"No, thanks."

"Good for you, Speed. I admire a fellow who doesn't smoke."

"Why don't you quit, then?"

"Oh, I could, but I enjoy it too much."

They reached brick-paved First Avenue and crossed the car tracks to the other side. Halfway down the block the fellow stopped in front of an establishment with "RAFFERTY'S TABLE BOARD" lettered on the window. A card beneath it read, "All you can eat for 50c." He waved a hand toward the door. "This is it."

"Thanks for showing me."

"Best grub in town." He sniffed at the aroma coming from the entrance. "Mmmm, does that smell good!"

Vic hesitated. "Well, thanks."

The fellow just stood there, halfway blocking the door, looking through the window at the tables with the chairs around them. There were several men inside, eating. "Boy, look at those guys shovel it in," he said. His shoulders sagged and he started to walk away. "I guess I'd better go on home and have some beans. So long, Speed. Nice knowin' you."

Vic started to pull the door open. "Well, uh . . . why don't you come on in, too? I've got enough for both of us."

"You know, Speed, the minute I saw you in that line this morning I knew you was a good scout."

"You have to pay in advance, boys," the man behind the cash register said crisply. "Fifty cents apiece, please."

Vic dug down and handed over the silver dollar Mr. Frank had given him. The cashier rang it up, gave them each a ticket and waved toward the tables. "I can see I'm gonna lose money on you boys, but a deal's a deal. Hop to it."

They took seats at the table nearest the kitchen. Vic hung his coat over the back of the chair and put his gunny sack on the floor. He looked at his hands. "I wonder if they've got a place here where you can wash up?"

His companion nodded toward a door at the rear of the room. "Right in there. I'll keep an eye on your stuff."

When Vic came back from the men's room a waitress was setting a kettle of soup and a dish of oyster crackers on the red-checkered tablecloth. "Vegetable soup today, boys," she said, "and it's good. Eat lots."

"Don't worry," Vic said, "we will." He ladled a bowl full and pushed the kettle across the table. "Here, have some—say, what's your name, anyway?"

The fellow took some soup before answering. "Uh .. George Brown."

George Brown? Vic was sure that wasn't the name he'd given the CCC clerk. But maybe he was wrong. "I'm Vic Martin."

"Glad to know you."

Vic began to eat. "Boy, this soup is good."

"Yeah, but go easy on it," George said. "That's the way Rafferty makes his money. He wants you to fill up on soup and crackers, then you won't eat too much meat and spuds."

"Don't worry."

Vic ate two bowls of soup and would have taken more but George stopped him. "As long as you keep inhalin' soup they won't bring us anything else." He turned and yelled to the waitress, "Hey, we're done with this soup! Bring on the grub!"

She came, took away the soup, brought bread, coffee, a bowl of boiled potatoes, a kettle of beef stew and two slabs of apple pie. "This is more like it," George said, heaping his plate.

Vic agreed and filled his own.

The boys wolfed the food down and Vic was reaching for his second helping when he looked up and saw two thin-faced, shabbily dressed men and an old woman looking in through the front window. They were watching every bite he took. Suddenly he wasn't as hungry as he had been.

"That *was* a meal!" George said when the pie was gone. He patted his stomach. "We never see anything like that at home. Why, you'd think those dames at the welfare board had to pay for the stuff they give you with their own money." He began feeling in his pockets. "By golly, I guess I ain't got a cig left to my name." He drummed his fingers on the table for a moment. "Say, Speed, how about bein' a real good sport and let me borrow a dime so I can get a pack of Wings?"

"Well, I'm kind of short, George, and . . ."

"You're not gonna turn out to be a piker now, are you?"

Vic handed over a dime.

"Now I know you're all right, Speed." George went to the cashier's desk and bought a pack of cigarettes while Vic put on his mackinaw.

The people were still looking in through the restaurant window. As they came out, one of the men approached Vic with his hat in his hand. "Say, Mister, I wonder if you could spare . . ."

Vic reached into his pocket and George caught him by the arm. "I wouldn't give that bum a cent if I was you."

Vic shook off his hand and gave the man a dime.

"Come on, let's get out of here." George hurried Vic along as other men started in their direction. "It doesn't do any good to give those panhandlers anything, Speed. He'll probably spend that dime for beer."

"What do you mean?" Vic said. "That man's not a drunk, he's hungry."

George did not reply, but when they got to the corner he said, "Do you want me to show you some of the hot spots? I know where they all are."

Vic hesitated. "Well, uh . . . thanks, George, but it's kind of late. I've got to find a place to sleep tonight."

48

"You can get a bed in a flophouse for a quarter and there's fleabag hotels around that only charge half a dollar, but I wouldn't recommend them to my worst enemy." George thought for a moment, then slapped Vic on the back. "Say, I just had a bright idea, Speed. Why don't we go down there to the Green Parrot Theater and get a couple of tickets? We can see the show and afterward you can curl up in your seat and sleep for the rest of the night. If we go in before five it will only cost a dime apiece and you sure can't get a room for that."

"Do they let you stay all night?"

"Everybody does it."

They went to the theater. George pointed to the colored posters on the front of the building. "Look, Speed, Tom Mix in a Western and Lon Chaney in a horror movie. What a bill!" He prodded Vic to the box office.

Vic bought two tickets with his paper dollar and the cashier gave him back a fifty-cent piece and three dimes. Except for the few pennies in his pocket and the dollar he was saving for a ferry ticket, this was all he had. And if he didn't get rid of George Brown pretty soon he wouldn't have anything.

He gave the tickets to the doorman and they stepped inside. The theater smelled of stale tobacco smoke and unwashed people wearing unclean clothes. But it was warm. A trimly uniformed girl with a flashlight showed them to their seats and Vic put his bag on the floor. The horror movie was in progress. It was

soon over and the Western started. When Tom Mix
had disposed of the last Indian, the lights came on
and peddlers walked down the aisles selling refresh-
ments. "What do you say we get us a couple of ice
cream sandwiches," George suggested.

"I'm getting low on cash."

"They're only a nickel apiece. You ain't gonna get
cheap for a measly dime, are you?"

Vic bought the sandwiches.

The lights went out again and a newsreel flashed
on. There was applause for President Franklin D.
Roosevelt giving his Easter message to the nation.
There was a shot of the wreckage of the dirigible
"Akron" floating on the Atlantic Ocean, and scenes
showing people in various parts of the country drinking legal beer for the first time since 1920. The newsreel was followed by a Charley Chase comedy, then
Lon Chaney came on again in the horror movie. Vic
had seen enough of that, so he slid down in his seat,
stretched his legs, and went to sleep.

"Salted peanuts, ice cream sandwiches! Chewing
gum, cigarettes!"

Vic blinked as the lights came on at the end of the
Tom Mix show and the peddlers again began moving
up and down the aisles.

A dim-faced clock above the screen showed the
time to be eleven-thirty. The theater was almost filled
with people who were sleeping or sitting, heavy-lid-
ded, waiting for the lights to go out again. As a ped-

dler came by, Vic reached in his pocket for a coin to buy a bag of peanuts and his hand went right on through. Someone had slit the cloth! He felt for his bag. It was gone, too! He shook his seat-mate. "Hey, George, somebody's robbed me!"

"What the devil's the matter with you?" a strange voice grumbled.

"Oh, sorry. Where did the guy go who was in that seat?"

"How should I know?" The stranger changed position, dropped his whiskery chin on his chest, and went back to sleep.

Vic jumped up and started for the exit. Then he went back to his seat. George Brown, or whatever his name was, was probably home in bed by this time, asleep or chortling over how he'd taken a country boy to the cleaners.

He felt in his shirt pocket and was reassured by the crumple of the paper there. The smartest thing he'd done all day had been to separate that dollar from the rest of his money. He never thought he'd have to use it so soon but he didn't have much choice now. It was back to the Peninsula for him. First thing in the morning he'd start for Edmonds, and once he got back to the other side he'd be among friends again. He'd go to Port Angeles and make a try at getting in the CCC there. And if he was turned down, he could always go back home. It would be a last resort, though, and he didn't like to think about it.

The lights went out and the newsreel began again

with the sound turned down so low that you could hardly hear it. That was considerate of the management, Vic thought, since most of the patrons were obviously more interested in sleep than they were in the show. He made himself as comfortable as he could and closed his eyes.

5

Vic was wakened by the cleaning men who came down the aisles calling, "Everybody out, everybody out so we can clean her up, boys!" The lights were on and the clock over the darkened screen read half past five.

Vic stretched and yawned and got stiffly to his feet and followed the drowsy men straggling toward the lobby. He felt grimy and had a fuzzy taste in his mouth and a slight headache. He went to the rest room and washed in cold water, rinsed his mouth, and tried to smooth his hair down with his wet hands. His comb and toothbrush had been in the gunny sack.

He was reluctant to leave the warmth of the theater, but once he was out on the wet and windy street and had a breath or two of fresh air, his headache went away. He hadn't realized how stuffy it had been inside. The men who'd spent the night with him wandered off in different directions. Vic wondered what they did during the day and how they fed themselves.

Over on the Peninsula if you were broke you could catch a fish or dig some clams, snare a rabbit, or pick some mushrooms, but what did you do in a city?

Right now his problem was to get to the ferry in Edmonds, the sooner the better. As he passed Rafferty's he looked in the window and eyed the stacks of pancakes, the plates of ham and eggs and fried potatoes, the bowls of mush and cups of coffee. Most of the breakfasters seemed to be workingmen with dinner buckets. Vic fingered his paper dollar, but hurried on.

Two blocks up the street he ran head-on into the delicious fragrance of hot coffee coming from a small shop with a window full of golden doughnuts, maple bars, and butter-horns. He didn't even hesitate, but grabbed the door handle and went in. "How much are your doughnuts?" he asked.

"The fresh ones are two for a nickel or two bits a dozen, but I've got some day-old ones you can have for fifteen cents a dozen."

"I'll take the day-old ones." As the clerk filled a sack from a tray beneath the counter, Vic asked, "How much is coffee?"

"Five cents."

"I'd better have a cup." He handed over the dollar, and was about to drop the change into his slit pocket when he caught himself, and put it into the other pocket. He sat down on a stool, put lots of sugar and cream in the coffee, and began to dunk a doughnut. He ate three, and the clerk refilled his cup for nothing.

When it was emptied he tucked the sack of doughnuts inside his shirt and went out again into the drizzle.

The deep notes of a steam whistle announced the arrival of a big freighter. This was something he wanted to see, a ship being berthed. He trotted down the hill, his hobnails clattering on the sidewalk, and crossed the railroad tracks and the splintery plank roadway built on pilings. He followed some men hurrying toward the dock from up and down the waterfront. His spirits rose. Maybe there was work to be had on this freighter. Maybe he could even ship out on her!

There was a crowd ahead of him, bunched around the gate barring the entrance to the pier. He walked up and spoke to a heavy-set man with a steel hook sticking out of his hip pocket. "How does a guy go about getting a job on a ship?"

The big man looked him over. "You're just off a farm, ain't you?" he said in a rasping voice.

"That's right."

"Let me tell you somethin' about the waterfront, Slim, just so you won't go gettin' yourself hurt. In the first place you ain't got enough beef on your bones to hold your own in a hatch, and in the second place you ain't wearin' no union button." He pointed toward the wall-like hull inching near. "There's four holds in that ship and countin' winch drivers and hatch tenders and stevedores and slingmen on the dock, they won't be needin' more than forty men to unload her—and our boys are goin' to do it."

"I don't want to help unload. I want to ship out."

"You ain't got A.B.'s papers, have you?"

"No."

"Or a lifeboat ticket?"

"No."

"They won't even let you up the gangway." The longshoreman jerked a thumb toward the city. "You'd be better off if you mosied on up the street. With all these scabs hangin' around, things might get a little rough."

Now there were at least two hundred men pressing toward the gate. Vic got out of the crowd, went off a little distance and leaned against a railing to watch the docking. Lines were heaved from the deck and made fast to bollards on the pier, and the great overhanging bow came to a silent stop a few feet from where he stood. The tugs cast off and backed out of the slip. A gangplank was swung out over the ship's rail and lowered by a cable leading through a block on a winged-out boom.

A man wearing a raincoat came out of an office on the dock, carrying a clipboard in his hand. He unlocked the gate and as the stevedore gangs started through, a group of bystanders tried to go in with them. A scuffle began; fists flew, and a man went down. Two men left the crowd, one with a bloody handkerchief to his nose, the other with a blackened eye.

"Just a bunch of thugs," one of them muttered as they went by. "All I want is a chance to earn enough to feed my kids and what do I get for it—a bust in the nose."

Vic hurried away. He cut across the plank roadway and started walking up the railroad tracks. There was a whistle behind him. He looked back and saw a freight train coming, traveling in the direction he wanted to go.

This was as good a way to get to Edmonds as any and probably the quickest. The train wasn't moving very fast and he had plenty of time to see the people in the empty boxcars behind the engine. They stood in the doorways, sat with their backs to the walls or stretched out sleeping on the floors.

Vic stepped up close to the tie ends, and as a gondola car came along he made a grab for the ladder at the front end. His fingers slipped on the rain-wet iron and he missed his hold. A moment later the rear of the car came by and he made a grab at the ladder there. He thought his arms were going to be yanked from their sockets as suddenly his feet were jerked from the ground and he was whipped around into the space between the cars. He got a foot on the air hoses under the couplers and reached for the next rung of the ladder with his left hand. He couldn't quite grab it and the other hand was weakening. He looked down and saw the rail passing beneath him and heard the grinding of the wheels.

He began clawing desperately for a hold and didn't see three blackened faces look over the edge of the car. A grimy hand shot down and caught him by the wrist,

57

another got hold of the collar of his mackinaw. There was a heave and he was standing upright on the narrow ledge at the end of the car. "Thanks!" he gasped.

The three faces belonged to two boys in their teens, badly in need of haircuts, and a bald, unshaven older man. Their hands and faces and ragged clothing were covered with coal dust left from the load the gondola car had once carried.

The older man spoke. "Didn't anybody ever tell you never to grab the hind end of a car?"

Vic was still gasping for breath. "This is the first time I ever tried it."

"And doggone near your last, too. When you reach for a rear-end grabiron you're asking to get cut in two. Next time you hop a freight on the fly, try for a front end."

Vic looked at his trembling hands. "There s not going to be any next time."

"Where you heading?"

"Just a few miles up the Sound."

"Local boy out for a ride, huh?"

"Yes. Where are you from?"

"We're just getting in from Starvationburg."

"Where?"

"Portland. How's the pickings in this town?"

"How's the what?"

"Handouts—chow, eats, chuck."

Vic reached inside his shirt. "If you guys are hungry I've got a few doughnuts here. They're a little stale but you're welcome to them."

The older man took the sack. "Manna from heaven!" He passed the doughnuts around to his companions and bit into one himself. "Why, they're as fresh as the morning dew." He offered Vic one. "Will you join us?"

"I've already had some."

The sack was passed around again. "I wish all our grub came as easy as this," one said.

"How do you fellows get by, anyway?" Vic asked.

"I ain't missed a meal yet," one of the boys said, "but some of them were a long way in between." The doughnuts came his way again; he took the last one. Vic noticed how carefully he smoothed the sack, folded it and put it in a pocket.

The area of docks and street crossings was left behind and the train picked up speed as it skirted the edge of the bay. Offshore, to the left, ships with rusty hulls and dirty paintwork swung at anchor, and all along the beach people were picking up bits of driftwood left by the receding tide.

The train passed under a bridge and the double set of tracks split into four, the four into eight, then split and split again, becoming a switching yard.

As far as Vic could see, the flat area between two hills was filled with freight cars and passenger coaches, engines and cabooses. With a hiss of escaping air and brake shoes grinding against wheel rims, the train shuddered to a stop. The bald hobo looked around. "Good old Interbay. She hasn't changed a bit." He threw a leg over the side of the gondola and went down the grabirons to the ground. His young traveling companions followed and Vic was right behind.

"Where's the jungle,* Curly?" one of the boys asked.

"There used to be a pretty good one up there the other side of the roundhouse. Come on, Slim, let's get out of here. The railroads don't mind us riding their trains but they don't like us hanging around the yards."

Like the other men they left by the most direct route, straight across the tracks to the nearest street. There were at least a hundred hobos, some with packsacks on their backs or bulky bedrolls on their shoulders. Most of them had nothing but the clothes they wore and whatever they might be carrying in their pockets.

"What are you guys going to do now?" Vic asked.

"Go to the jungle and get cleaned up," Curly said. "You can't go hitting back doors looking like a tramp."

Vic trailed along behind them.

The jungle was down over an embankment, in a clump of trees at the edge of a marsh just behind the roundhouse. Here, several hundred men stood or squatted by small fires or huddled under shelters made of tin and cardboard and scraps of lumber. The trees protected the area from the wind, but the rain dripping from the leaves fell hissing into the flames and turned the ground to mud. Most of the campfires

* See glossary at end of book for definitions of hobo terms and expressions.

60

look almost human again, Blackie," Billie said. "How do I look?"

"You'll get by."

With the grime and coal dust gone, the boys appeared even younger than Vic had believed them to be. Billie had curly red hair and a heavy sprinkling of freckles on his turned-up nose. He might have been sixteen, but he was small for his age and could have passed for a twelve-year-old if you didn't look at his eyes too closely or listen to him talk. Those eyes didn't miss anything, and when he spoke he left no doubt that he thought he knew exactly what he was talking about.

Blackie was older and taller, with black hair, a dark complexion, and deep brown eyes. He apparently hadn't started shaving yet but was going to have to soon. He was more relaxed than Billie and smiled more easily.

Vic had finished his own washing and was slicking down his hair when he noticed Billie eying the left front pocket of his tight-fitting overalls. He glanced down and saw his fifty-cent piece and three dimes outlined sharply against the thin and faded denim. "Did you rob a bank or something?" Billie asked.

"Oh, that's for my ferry ticket so I can get home."

Blackie took a step forward. "Maybe you'd better let us take care of it for you."

Vic planted his feet in the cinders and clenched his fists in front of him. "I can take care of it myself."

63

"Sure you can," Billie said. "Just stash it where no-body can see it."

Vic took the money from his pants and put it in his shirt pocket.

"You better spread it around so it won't clink, Slim. There's guys on the road who'd bash your head in for a nickel."

Vic put a coin in each of four different pockets. After last night's experience in the theater he should have thought to do that in the first place.

Billie looked around. "What do you know about this burg? We've never been here before."

"I never saw it until yesterday either."

"Then we're going to have to figure it out for ourselves." He surveyed the hill to the west.

"There's plenty of houses up there," Blackie said. "The smoke's starting to come out of the chimneys. We'll just about catch them when they're sitting down to breakfast."

Billie shook his head. "Yeah, but it's too close to the yards. The boes have probably got all the back doors up there beat half off their hinges already." He turned his attention the other way, east of the railroad yards. "That big hill over there is steep enough to make it hard to get to. We should have better luck up there."

"There's sure a lot of nice-looking houses up on that hill," Vic said.

"Don't let 'em fool you, Slim," Billie said. "Big houses and fresh paint means rich people, and they wouldn't give you their garbage."

64

"And that's why they're rich," Blackie said. "You're better off looking for little houses with no paint on them. The poor people know what it's like to be hard up and they're nearly always good for a handout."

"And that's why they're poor; they give everything away," Billie said. "I'm lookin' for somethin' halfway in between, some place where the workin' people live. What I want is a street far enough from the yards so too many boes haven't been around, where the houses aren't too big and they keep their lawns trimmed and there's cars in the driveways and curtains in the windows. Most people in places like that are gettin' by all right and it won't hurt them any to give you a spud or a couple of carrots."

"And they're more liable to be ashamed to turn you down."

Billie agreed. "I think if we get a few blocks back from those big houses on top of that hill we just might find some good pickin's. Come on, that boilin'-up can won't wait forever."

6

A rickety footbridge took them across the swampy ground behind the roundhouse to a road that led to a wide avenue with car tracks down the center. They crossed and found a steep side street that went up the hill beyond. Most of the houses at the foot of the hill had signs on gates and porches, warning "NO BUMS ALLOWED" or "NO HANDOUTS."

"Somebody's sure wore out our welcome around here," Billie said.

Halfway up the hill they stopped to rest their legs and get their breath. On the network of tracks in the yards below they could see switch engines breaking old trains apart and making up new ones. A forest of masts marked a fishing boat moorage close to the drawbridge that spanned the ship canal. Even from this distance they could see men picking through the refuse in a garbage dump near the railroad yards.

"What are those guys doing down there?" Vic asked.

"Hunting for their breakfast," Blackie answered.

"Curly's goin' to be wonderin' what's become of us," Billie said.

They started out again.

"Why didn't he come along?" Vic asked.

"Older guys don't have much luck bummin'. Folks think they ought to be workin', even if there ain't no work."

"Most women will feel sorry for a kid at their back door asking for a bite to eat," Blackie said. "Why, I've even had them invite me in to sit down at the table with them."

"You're the guy that falls into deals like that. It never happens to me."

"Maybe it's because I'm better looking than you."

"Does Curly just sit around the jungle while you guys do all the hustling?" Vic asked.

"Don't worry, Curly does his share," Blackie said. "He's always got a campin' spot staked out and a tin can on the fire when we get back. And he's teaching us the ropes, too. A kid can't just start out on his own."

"Sometimes I wish Curly didn't have such an itchy foot," Billie said. "I'd like to settle down for a while sometime."

"Your foot is just as itchy as his. And so is mine."

"Is that all you guys do," Vic asked, "just roam around from place to place?"

"That's right," Blackie said, "like Old Man River, we jest keep rollin'."

"Where all have you been?"

"About everywhere. We've done twenty thousand miles in the last year, Slim. Seen every state now but Idaho and Montana, and we'll be there soon."

"You ever work?"

"Why, sure. We're workin' right now."

"I mean get a job, earn money."

Billie grinned.

The street leveled abruptly and they hurried through a district of fine houses with tall hedges and ornamental shrubbery that rimmed the top of the hill.

"You don't hang around a neighborhood like this any longer than you have to," Billie said. "Everybody's got a phone to call cops with."

A few blocks away and out of sight of the view of Puget Sound and the Olympics, the houses were more modest. There were no warning signs on the doors and gates, the dogs were friendlier, and the faces at the windows were more curious than hostile. Potato plants grew in many of the parking strips and some of the houses had vegetable gardens in front instead of lawns. Thin green lines on the brown earth showed where rows of beets and carrots were pushing through the soil, and tendrils of young pea vines were reaching up to strings.

They stopped behind a boarded-up service station and Billie looked up and down the quiet street. "This looks like as good a place as any to start," he said.

"And we're just about right on time, too," Blackie said. "The men should be gone to work and the kids haven't left for school yet. There ought to be a lot of breakfast leftovers still sitting on the tables. Do you want me to work up the street, Billie?"

"Yeah, and me 'n' ol' Slim here will go down the street. We'll meet you back here in about half an hour."

Blackie walked off up the street whistling.

Billie started to go in the other direction. "Come on, Slim."

Vic hung back. "Maybe you'd better count me out. I've never done anything like this before."

"Aw, come on! You're a natural for this racket, Slim."

"What do you mean?"

"Why, you're so skinny you look like you ain't et for a month. People will give you stuff just to keep you from droppin' dead on their doorsteps."

"Maybe, but I just can't go up and knock on somebody's door and ask for something to eat."

"If you get hungry enough you will."

"I'm plenty hungry right now but I don't think I can do it."

"All right." Billie's voice sharpened. "But don't think you can come back to the jungle and expect to get in on our mulligan when we get it built. Them that don't work don't eat."

"How do I go about it? What do I ask for?" Vic asked.

"Go around to the back door and tap just loud enough for 'em to hear you. When they open up, stand back and smile and ask if they've got some work you can do to earn a potato or an onion to put into a stew you're going to make."

"Just one potato?"

"Everybody can spare just one spud and they'll probably give you a couple." They started down the street. Billie pointed to a big white house in the middle of the block. "That looks like a good prospect, Slim. Go on up and knock."

"Why don't you do it at this first place and I'll watch."

Billie frowned. "Two guys don't have near the chance that just one does, but we'll give it a try."

They opened the gate, and as they started down the walk that led to the back of the house Vic began to tremble. "My mom would slaughter me if she knew I was going begging," he said.

"She'll never know unless you tell her." Billie stopped by the corner of the house. "Now, I'll go up and knock and you—what are you shakin' for, you're not scared, are you?"

"You bet I'm scared."

"They won't any more than slam the door in our faces, or sic a dog on us."

"Or call the cops."

"Boy, you're pale. You look sick, Slim."

"I feel sick."

"Good, that ought to get their sympathy. Put on a long face and try to look real miserable." Billie went up and tapped lightly on the door while Vic stood at the bottom of the steps. He didn't have to *try* to look miserable.

Billie tapped again, harder. A moment later the face of a plump, motherly-looking middle-aged woman appeared at the window. She opened the door a crack and Billie said, "Lady, my brother's not feelin' very good. I wonder if you could spare a couple of aspirin tablets?"

"What's the matter, has he got the grippe?"

"Could be—he's been shakin' like that since last night."

What a fibber that kid is, Vic thought.

"Where do you boys live?"

"We just came up from the railroad yards, Ma'am."

"Hobos, eh?" Her eyes flicked from one to the other. "You certainly don't look like brothers."

"Oh, we are, Ma'am. Half brothers, that is."

A real first class fibber.

"Why aren't you home and in school where you belong?"

"We've got no home, Ma'am."

"Oh." She beckoned to Vic. "Come up here and let me look at you." He came up the steps and she felt his forehead. "No fever." She felt his wrist. "Pulse a bit fast. Let me see your tongue." He put it out. "Hmmm."

"I feel better now," Vic said. "Let's go." He started down the steps.

Billie caught him by the sleeve. "He always gets

pale and shakes like that when he hasn't et for a couple of days, Ma'am."

She nodded. "I know just what he needs." She went back into the house.

Billie nudged Vic and whispered, "That sick brother and no-home business gets 'em every time."

The lady returned with a large spoon and a bottle containing a clear, thick substance. She filled the spoon. "Take this."

"Uh . . . what is it?"

She thrust the spoon into Vic's mouth. "Boys your age seldom get anything wrong with them that a good dose of castor oil won't cure." She smiled. "I've raised six of my own."

Vic gagged as he swallowed the sticky, foul-tasting oil. Billie began to snicker and the lady filled the spoon again. "You might be catching the same thing your brother has." She shoved it into Billie's half-open mouth. "It certainly won't hurt you and it will probably do you a lot of good." She started back into the house. "Now, you boys . . ."

They didn't wait to hear the rest. Billie hurried down the steps and around the corner of the house, with Vic right behind. They were still spitting when they reached the sidewalk. "I wish I had a piece of chalk," Billie growled. "I'd put the 'no good' mark on her gate."

"What's that?"

"It's to warn the other boes to stay away from the

place." Billie spat again. "The least she could have done was give us a cup of coffee to wash the taste out of our mouths."

"What do we do now?"

"Keep hustlin'." Billie opened a gate.

"Do I have to come with you?"

"You better not, you're a hoodoo. I'm goin' by myself." He started down the walk toward the back of the house.

Vic walked on up the street. He wanted to get in on the mulligan but he was more reluctant than ever to knock on a back door.

There was a grocery store on the corner and through the window Vic could see the aproned grocer arranging vegetables on a rack, preparing for the day's business. Behind the meat counter a butcher, wearing a straw hat and with paper cuffs around his wrists, had a quarter of beef on the block, working at it with saw and knife and cleaver. The sight of the big slabs of red meat made Vic's mouth water.

The butcher began trimming off bits of suet and bone and tossing them into a box on the sawdust-covered floor.

Vic felt for one of his dimes. He'd probably have just as much trouble getting aboard the ferry with eighty cents as he would with only seventy. He went in and walked up to the showcase full of steaks and wieners, roasts and sausages.

"Good morning," the butcher said. "Kind of nippy out, isn't it?"

"Sure is." Vic put his dime down and nodded toward the box of trimmings on the floor. "Could I buy . . . how many of those scraps will you give me for ten cents? I've got a dog . . ."

The butcher looked at him for a moment. Then he put down his knife, spread out a piece of brown paper and put several large bones on it. He cut a chunk of solid meat from the end of the quarter and threw it on the pile.

He wrapped the package and shoved it across the counter, but when Vic slid the dime toward him, he shook his head and shoved the money back. "No charge, son."

"Gee, thanks."

"Don't mention it." The butcher went back to trimming meat.

On his way out Vic passed the vegetable stand. The grocer popped open a large sack and began putting vegetables into it.

"I've got a few things here your dog might like, too. The carrots are a little wilted and the potatoes are starting to sprout, but there's nothing else the matter with them." He handed the sack to Vic, who tried to give him the dime.

"Keep your money, kid. This is stuff I'd have to throw out anyway." He reached under the bakery shelf. "And here's a loaf of day-old bread he might like to chew on, too."

Vic went out the door with his arms loaded and feeling as if he'd just inherited a million dollars. But he knew he hadn't fooled them a bit with his story about a dog.

Ahead, he saw Billie coming out of a yard, muttering to himself.

"How are you making out?" Vic asked when they met at the boarded-up service station.

Billie looked around. "No good a-tall. Why, this town is as bad as—hey, whatcha got there?"

Vic grinned. "Soup bones, meat, carrots, spuds . . ."

Billie looked into the sack. "You even got a loaf of bread. What did you do, spend all that money you had?"

Vic shook his head. "No, I just went in and laid a dime on the counter and told them I wanted some bones for my dog."

A block away they saw Blackie coming around the corner and waved to him. He shrugged his shoulders and spread his empty hands. "I guess he didn't do so good, either," Billie said. He pointed to Vic's packages, making eating motions, and Blackie increased his pace. "Say," Billie said, "I'm gonna have some fun with ol' Blackie when he gets here. Now let me do the talkin' and you agree with everything I say."

"Okay."

"What did you birds do, anyway?" Blackie asked when he arrived. "Knock over a grocery store?"

Billie slapped Vic on the back. "Blackie, this kid's a wonder. He walks into a meat market and asks for bones for his dog and they give him half the joint. It's his bein' so skinny that did it."

"Well, I'm glad somebody made a good touch. I didn't even get a nibble."

"You haven't heard anything yet, Blackie. The very first house we hit the old gal takes one look at Slim and whips us up a batch of flapjacks and bacon and eggs."

"No kiddin'?"

"I can still taste it, can't you, Slim?"

"I sure can."

"I'll bet if you went there she'd give you some of the same thing, Blackie."

Billie took Blackie by the arm and led him away from the side of the service station. "See that big white house up there in the middle of the block? Go give it a try. I'd hate to see you miss out on a cinch deal like that."

"Are you sure there's not some catch to it?"

"We didn't have to split wood or anything, did we, Slim?"

Vic shook his head.

"Okay, I'll have a go at it." Blackie headed up the street.

"Be sure and tell her you're not feelin' good. She's the sympathetic type."

When he was out of earshot, Vic said, "That was a dirty trick."

"What do you mean, a dirty trick? A dose of castor oil won't hurt him and it'll probably do him some good." Billie got a devilish gleam in his eye. "And besides, this will pay him back for some of the stunts he's pulled on me."

"What do you say we have a slice or two of this bread while we're waiting for him?" Vic said.

"Nothin' doin'. We don't touch any of that stuff till we get back to the jungle and divide it up with Curly."

"It's my loaf of bread. The man gave it to me."

"We don't figure it that way, Slim. If somebody gives you somethin' on a plate it's all right to eat it. Anything that's in a sack or you can put in your pocket you've got to save and split with your buddies. That's one of the rules of the road."

"How do you know they divide everything they get with you?"

"Gosh, Slim, if a fellow has to be watched all the time he ain't worth havin' around." Billie pointed up the street. "Oh, oh, here he comes already." He chuckled. "That didn't take him long."

"Look, he's got a sack in his hand."

Blackie was whistling "Happy Days" as he came near. "Boy, you sure were right when you said she was a soft touch."

"What did she give you anyway?" Billie asked, eying the sack.

Blackie opened it and they looked in. "Some sandwiches, a couple of oranges, and two pieces of cake."

"Is that *all* she gave you?"

"Sure, what more do you want?"

"It certainly didn't take you long."

"You know, it's a funny thing, the lady had them already made up. She said two guys were there a little while ago trying to get something to eat. She went in to fix it for them and when she came out they were gone."

7

A hundred heads turned and a hundred pairs of eyes focused on the sacks that Vic and Blackie carried through the jungle to Whitey's fire. Curly was squatting on his heels sipping from a tin can. "You're just in time for coffee, lads. Help yourself to the gunboat."

Billie and Blackie took empty soup cans from their coat pockets and dipped them into the gunboat steaming on the hot rocks beside the boilin'-up can. "Who do we owe for this?" Billie asked.

Curly nodded to a little man standing on the other side of the fire with Whitey. "Shorty's your host."

"Thanks, Shorty."

The little man grinned. "How about you, Slim, going to have a little java with us?"

"I don't have anything to put it in."

Curly drained his can. "You can use mine." He refilled the can and handed it to Vic. "Here, let me take that sack."

"Slim's a wizard," Billie said. "His very first touch he gets everything for a mulligan, includin' bones an' some meat, too."

Blackie held out his sack. "I got some sandwiches and fruit."

"Good. We'll save that for traveling chuck." Curly opened the butcher's package. "*Real* meat!" He took off the shingle that was being used as a lid for the boilin'-up can, dumped everything in and put the shingle back on.

"Boy, I can't remember how long it's been since I was in on a mulligan that had meat in it," Blackie said.

"A month, anyhow," Billie guessed.

"Slim, you're a natural," Curly said. He took out a pocket knife and began removing the thinnest of parings from a carrot. "Where'd you say you were heading?"

"Back to the Olympic Peninsula."

"What's over there?"

"I'm going to try to get into one of those CCC camps the Government is starting up."

"What if you don't make it?"

Vic took a sip of his coffee, then shrugged. "I don't know. Go home, I guess. I came over to try to join the Navy but they're not taking any enlistments now."

Curly sliced the carrots into the boilin'-up can. "Decide you want to see the world or something?"

"That was part of it, I guess."

"You don't have to be in the Navy to see the world."

Curly reached for a potato and began to peel it carefully. "Did you ever think of going on the road?"

Vic shook his head. "I don't think I'd like it."

"It's an honorable profession."

"But I like to eat too well."

Curly lifted the shingle and threw the potato into the boilin'-up can. "A couple of hours and you'll be eating as well as anybody."

Vic had his doubts. A handful of bones and suet and a little bit of meat, a few wilted carrots and potatoes in a five-gallon can half full of water—that was going to be a mighty thin stew. But anything would taste good by the time it was cooked. The aroma wafting through the jungle from the boilin'-up can soon attracted attention. A man with thick gray hair came up to the fire, sniffing. "How about helpin' out on the mulligan, fellas?" he said.

"What have you got?" Curly asked.

The newcomer produced an onion. "Will this do?"

"If you got two of 'em, it will. We got meat here, you know."

The man took another from his pocket.

"Pull up a chair." Curly peeled the onions and sliced them into the can.

Shorty nodded toward the gunboat. "Have some coffee?"

"Thanks." The newcomer filled his drinking can and squatted on his heels before the fire.

Other hungry men came along with more vegetables

for the mulligan. One had coffee to add to the gunboat, and another passed around his tobacco can for
everyone who wanted to roll a smoke. Still another
brought an armful of wood and was allowed to join
the group.

Curly fed the fire carefully. Occasionally he would
lift the shingle, peer in and stir the mulligan with a
stick. The can was almost filled now with the con-
tributions of a dozen men. Curly improvised a song:

"Oh, the man who's king in hobo land,
    Is the guy who tends the boilin'-up can."

An old, gray-muzzled dog, with ribs showing
through its skin, came sniffing toward the fire. Curly
snapped his fingers. "Come here, old-timer." The dog
came trembling to him. "Do you want to get in on the
mulligan?" The dog wagged its tail feebly. "You got to
help out, you know." The dog licked his hand. "That's
good enough."

With two sticks Curly fished a bone out of the can
and laid it on a board. "Any objections?" The men
around the fire shook their heads. When the bone had
cooled he gave it to the dog. The animal wagged its
tail, then went off beneath a bush and began to gnaw.
"Every inch a gentleman," Curly said, "and a first
class bo."

An engine left the roundhouse, backed up and
coupled onto a string of freight cars. "That must be

your local about to pull out now, Slim," Curly said. There was the blast of a whistle, the hiss of releasing air brakes, and the train began to creep forward. Vic started to leave. "Remember what I told you about grabbing onto the head end of a car," Curly warned. He lifted the shingle and stirred the mulligan.

"What do I do if it doesn't stop at Edmonds?"

"Just call the porter," Blackie said. "He'll have the conductor let you off."

The hobos guffawed.

"Jump off facing forward and light a-running," Curly said.

"And don't land on no switch," Billie warned, "or you'll rip your guts out and get a quick trip to the Big Rock Candy Mountain."

"Quick trip to where?"

"Heaven, paradise or whatever you want to call it."

"Oh. Well, don't worry." Vic paused, looked back at the boilin'-up can. "I wish that train would wait a little longer."

"It won't, but you can," Curly said. "Why don't you stick around, Slim? There's always another train."

Vic didn't reply, but he didn't hurry, either. He was too hungry to care. He stood at the foot of the embankment and watched the freight train gather speed. When the caboose had passed he came back and squatted by the fire.

About an hour after the train left, a whistle blew atop the roundhouse. "Must be noon." Curly took off the shingle, dipped the stirring stick, and tasted.

"Gentlemen, dinner is served." The men came with their cans and dipped them full of mulligan.

"Say, I need something to eat out of," Vic said.

"There's a Christmas tree over there with some cans hanging on it," Curly said. "Go help yourself."

Vic took an empty tomato can from a limb of the tree and filled it. A few of the hobos had spoons but the others drank the stew right out of their cans.

Curly served himself last. "Is there enough salt in it for you gentlemen?"

"Perfect!"

"You got a real good do on it, Curly."

"Yes, sir, right good," everyone agreed.

The cans were soon emptied and the men lined up for a refill. When the seconds were gone, too, Curly said, "There's about enough for one more round, boys."

"No more for me," Vic said. "I'm full to the gills."

"You better take it anyway, Slim. In this business you've got to be like a bear. When the grub's there, take it, because you don't know when you'll eat again."

Vic filled his can. "Okay, but I think I'll save it for later."

"Good idea."

Most of the others put their last helpings aside for later, too. When everything was gone but the bones, more water was brought from the roundhouse and the boilin'-up can was hung over the fire to heat again. "We'll see if we can get a little more mileage out of those bones," Curly said.

The tobacco was passed around and smokes were rolled and lighted. The can came to Vic and he passed it on to Billie, who deftly rolled a cigarette and gave the tobacco to Blackie.

When everyone was comfortable Curly said, "Well, lads, shall we stick around here a few days or move on?"

Billie took a deep drag on his cigarette. "I'd say move on."

"Yeah," Blackie agreed, "let's keep rolling."

"Okay, then let's take the eastbound manifest out of here tonight. Too bad you aren't going with us, Slim."

"We could sure have a lot of fun this summer, Slim," Blackie urged.

Vic hesitated. Rain running down his neck, muddy ground underfoot—he was used to such things. But he'd never gone hungry. Maybe there was nothing very fancy at home but when mealtime came, there was always something on the table, even if it was only clams or potatoes. And they'd never had to beg for it.

"Well thanks, anyway," he said finally. "Guess I'll go back to the Peninsula and give the CCC a try. If I don't make it this time, then—well . . ."

It was just beginning to be dark when a long drawn-out whistle came from the south, followed by the sound of an engine picking up speed. "That'll be the varnish comin' down the main line," someone said. Moments later they were blinded by a headlight, and a handsome engine pounded by with siderods flashing, steam spurting from the cylinder cocks. It was followed by several mail and baggage cars, and day coaches with people sitting in the lighted windows. The other cars of the passenger train were sleek Pullmans rolling by with stately smoothness. There was a momentary glimpse of well-dressed diners sitting on red leather chairs at tables with white cloths. "Boy, there's the way to travel," Blackie said.

"And they're payin' for it, too."

A sleeping car went by with a man lying on the top with his cap pulled down about his ears. In an instant he was out of sight. "That guy's not paying for it." Vic laughed.

"He'll pay for it before the night is over."

"Oh, they'll jerk him off at Everett. Somebody in the yards must've seen him goin' by."

"If he's *lucky* they'll jerk him off at Everett. It's no fun goin' over the hump this time of year, even in a boxcar."

"I wonder how that guy got aboard," someone said. "The station bulls watch those streaks of varnish like hawks."

"He probably dropped over the railing down there at Main Street when she went into the tunnel."

"He must want to get somewhere in a hurry," Vic said.

"Not necessarily." Curly shrugged. "There are boes that ride nothing but the varnish. It's a game with them, outsmarting the bulls."

"And there's guys that won't ride anything but Pullmans, too."

"Yeah, that's the hardest thing there is."

"Those sleepin' car conductors are real rough. If George Pullman don't get his cut, nobody gets aboard."

"You got to be a real man to hop a Pullman."

"Some day I'm going to ride the varnish," Blackie said.

"Boy, you can have it," said Billie. "I'll stick to side-door Pullmans. When I get on a train I want to be aboard when it gets to the end of the run."

"No, I mean I'll be inside, on the cushions."

"Whatcha gonna do, get a job as a newsie?"

"No, sir, I'll be paying." Blackie sounded sure.

But Billie snorted. "You and your big ideas."

"Don't they try to keep you off the freight trains, too?" Vic asked.

"Not now, but I remember the day when they did," Curly said.

With the approach of night, the wind sharpened and it began to rain harder. Vic turned his back to the weather and huddled closer to the fire, seeing in the flames the image of a man riding unprotected atop a speeding Pullman car. He hoped he would reach his destination safely. He tried to forget his own discomforts but couldn't help shivering from the cold. "I wonder when that freight train leaves?" he asked.

"Go up in the yard and ask one of the snakes," Curly said.

"One of the what?"

"Snakes—switchmen. And don't walk down the middle of the tracks. There's a lot of boxcars drifting around in the dark up there."

Vic went up the embankment and followed the sidetrack toward the roundhouse. He saw a light coming toward him. A workman materialized out of the darkness carrying a lantern and dinner bucket. He had a heavy black mustache and wore a slicker, rain hat, and rubber overshoes. He stopped when he saw Vic.

"Say, Mister, do you know when that eastbound freight train leaves?"

"She go about midnight," the man answered with a strong Italian accent.

"Thanks. What time is it now?"

The workman took out a heavy pocket watch and looked at it by the light of his lantern. "Eight o'clock."

"Th-thanks a lot." Vic's teeth were chattering.

The man held up the lantern and looked into his face. "Hey, you're just a kid!" He looked at Vic's trembling body. "How you like a nice warm place to stay till the train go?"

"Anything's better than this."

"You come with me, kid." Vic followed him to a small corrugated iron shed a short distance down the track. When the door was opened, a wave of warm air came out. The workman shone his lantern inside, and Vic saw a large stove with a metal hopper around it glowing in the center of a room that was knee-deep with sand.

"This is the sandhouse. You can sleep here." The workman put down his lantern and dinner bucket, opened the stove and threw in a shovelful of coal from a nearby bin.

Vic held his hands close to the heat and rubbed them together. "Say, Mister, you don't know how I appreciate this."

"That's all right. You a good kid. You not a smart aleck like lotta kids. I bet you're hungry, too."

Vic unbuttoned his coat to let the heat inside his damp clothing. "I'm always hungry."

The man opened his dinner bucket, took out a sandwich made from thick slices of brown bread with onions and salami in between. "Here, you eat this, boy."

"But that's part of your lunch."

"Oh, the old lady, she always fix too much." He shoved the sandwich into Vic's hands.

"Well, thanks, Mister."

The man snapped the lid back on his dinner bucket and picked up the lantern. "I come an' wake you up when the train goes." He went out and closed the door behind him.

The dancing firelight shone through the stove door, casting a rosy glow around the big sandwich that the workman had left. Vic wondered if the rules of the road about sharing applied here. The sandwich hadn't been on a plate but was handed to him. Did that amount to the same thing? If he tried to take it back to the jungle, unwrapped as it was, the rain would make a soggy mess of it. He could carry it underneath his coat, but it wouldn't give four of them much more than a bite each.

That wasn't the point, and Vic knew it. He lost the argument with himself and sank his teeth into the firm, sweet bread, munching the crunchy onion and the spicy, garlicky meat.

By the time the sandwich was gone he was really warm and steam was rising from his clothes. Here was something he *could* share with the others. He left the sandhouse, bowed his head into the wind and went back to the jungle. A lot of wood had been heaped on the fire, and at least twenty men were gathered around it when he got there.

"When does she leave, Slim?" Curly asked.

"About midnight." He beckoned to Curly and the boys, took them aside and told them about the sandhouse.

"You *are* a lucky one!" Curly turned and spoke to the men around the fire. "Come on, fellas, Slim's found a sandhouse for us to sleep in."

He started up the embankment and everybody left the fire and followed. Some called to men at other fires and they came along, too.

"What did you tell everybody for?" Vic whispered to Curly as they walked along by the tracks.

"Why not? They're cold and wet, too."

"But there isn't room for them all."

"Oh, no? You just watch!"

When somehow they had all crowded inside the sandhouse, Vic asked, "What do they use all this sand for, anyway?"

"The engines carry it," Curly said. "If the wheels start slipping on a hill they dump a little on the rails for traction."

"Why do they keep it in a hot place like this?"

"If it isn't dry it won't run through the pipes."

"Well, the heat sure feels good," Vic said. He moved a little to make room for a late-comer to squeeze in.

8

"Mama, mia! Where did all you fellas come from?"

The exclamation and the dazzle of a lantern shining in his face wakened Vic and he raised up on one elbow. "Hello," he said, looking toward the doorway. "Is it time to leave?"

"Not yet. I just come to put more coal in the stove. Come on, you fellas, move over so I can get in." A few of the boys squeezed over and made room for the workman. When he opened the stove door, the glowing coals lighted up a scene of tangled arms and legs. Muttering to himself as he tried to keep from stepping on anyone, the workman shoveled in some coal and slammed the door shut with a clang.

"What time is it now, Mister?" Vic asked.

"About half-pas' ten. You get some more sleep, boy. Don't worry, I wake you up in time." Picking up his lantern and stepping carefully over the sprawled-out bodies of the sleepers on the floor, he went out and closed the door behind him.

Vic didn't go back to sleep immediately but lay listening to the wind pelting rain against the metal walls. Between gusts he heard the water draining off the building onto the ground outside. The crowded room was getting stuffy and needed ventilation, but it was wonderfully warm and he wasn't looking forward at all to leaving it.

The fresh coal caught and the fire burned high. Now it was uncomfortably hot. By the flickering light of the flames shining through the drafts, Vic looked for a spot farther away from the stove, but all the space was taken, right up to the walls. So he settled down again. He might as well soak up all the heat he could because in a couple of hours he was going to need it.

He didn't really think that any hobo in his right mind would get up and leave a warm place like this to go out into a cold rain and climb aboard a freight train. But if Curly and the boys did go, he'd go with them. He bet, though, that they'd all still be here in the morning. There would always be another freight train. He burrowed his sharp hip bones down into the sand and went back to sleep.

It seemed he'd hardly closed his eyes when a cold draft blew in and the lantern was shining in his face again. "All right! You fellas that's-a go east, better get up now!"

Vic kept his eyes shut and pretended he didn't hear. Beside him he felt Curly stir and sit up, heard him yawn and say, "I guess that means us."

Vic felt a hand shaking him. "All right, Slim, rise and shine." Curly yawned again. "Billie! Blackie! Up and at 'em!" The boys roused, stretching and yawning.

Vic sat up and looked toward the open door. The workman stood just outside, holding his lantern so it would give light to those inside the sandhouse. His hat and slicker glistened, his face was wet and raindrops dripped from his big mustache.

"You're not really going out in this weather, are you?" Vic said.

"What's wrong with this?" Curly answered. "When there's a train to catch, we go."

They got to their feet and shook the sand out of their clothes. Vic stopped just outside the doorway. "Thanks a lot, Mister," he said to the workman.

"An' good luck to you, boy."

Vic followed Curly and the boys into the darkness, and crossed several sets of tracks to a big freight engine sighing on the main line.

"Looks like we've got a Malley on tonight," Billie said.

"She'll only be with us part way up the hill," Curly explained. "There's a long tunnel on this line where they can't use steam and they put on electrics for the run over the hump."

Outlined by floodlights mounted on the yard office,

the Malley, a compound locomotive with two sets of driving wheels, seemed a living monster with a single glaring eye. But a steam pump on the cowcatcher hissed a friendly, "Sh-shh, sh-shh," as though admonishing them to go by quietly. They felt a pleasant warmth as they drew nearer. But it was not entirely friendly. It spat scalding water at them as they passed a leaky valve, and the oil flame within the red-hot firebox made them hurry by to escape being seared. Vic jumped when the safety valve atop the boiler popped off.

They passed the cab where the engineer and fireman were checking valves and gauges. Behind the engine was the fuel and water tank, silent except for the high-pitched whine of an electric generator. Men with lanterns and wrenches were working at the coupler and hose lines that connected the engine to its train.

The first half dozen units were empty boxcars with side doors open. "Why don't we get in one of these?" Vic asked as Curly walked on by.

"These aren't for us," Curly replied. "They nearly always set the first ones off along the line someplace. We'll find one farther back." He stopped beside a gondola car. "You better get aboard this one, Slim, because if you have to get off on the fly, you'll never make it out of a boxcar."

"Isn't getting off on the fly kind of dangerous?"

"Not if you do it right. Get down on that stirrup at

the bottom of the ladder and drop off running. Take off away from the train, too. Then if you trip you won't wind up under the wheels."

"And what if the train's going too fast?"

"Stay aboard."

"These rattlers nearly always slow down going through a town," Blackie said.

"Hope you're right."

"Well, good luck, Slim," Curly said. "I wish you were going with us." They shook hands all around.

"You're sure going to miss a lot of fun," Blackie said. "But here's your share of the traveling chuck." There was the rustle of a paper sack as he took out several slices of dry bread and an orange and put them in Vic's hands. With mumbled thanks Vic shoved them into his pocket and reached for the ladder on the end of the car.

"Remember what I told you about not landin' on a switch," Billie said.

"So long, Slim," they called. "Take it easy."

"You, too!" Vic climbed up the wet grabirons, threw a leg over the top, and dropped down into the gondola.

In the short walk from the sandhouse to the train his clothes had been soaked again. Shivering, he huddled close to the end of the gondola where he got some shelter from the boxcar up ahead. He knew it would be worse when the train got under way.

He heard footsteps crunching in the cinder paths

between the railroad tracks on either side. Underneath the floodlights shadowy forms were going by, some with packs and some with nothing. He heard a voice say, "Let's see if there's some empties on down the line." There were more footfalls and more voices, then a laboring cough.

A sharp hiss came from underneath the car, followed by the creaking of a spring. Someone going by said, "Get a move on, Joe, they're bleedin' the brakes already." The engine whistled and in the darkness far down toward the rear end of the train, a lantern made an arc.

"Hurry it up, fellas," the same voice called, "they just gave the engineer the highball!" There was another whistle blast, then a "Huff-chuff!" from the engine's smokestack. From up ahead there came a rolling sound, like a row of toppling dominoes, as each car jerked the one next to it into motion. The sound grew louder, and Vic was almost thrown from his feet as the gondola jolted and began to roll.

Vic leaned over the side of his car and looked forward. Ahead was the upright arm of a semaphore. The signal light was green, and the headlight showed the tracks were clear. The train crawled past the yard office and the sandhouse. The mustached workman in his dripping rain hat and shining slicker was standing by a switch lamp watching. As he went by, Vic called down, "So long, Mister! Thanks for everything!"

The man held his lantern high, then his white teeth

showed in a broad smile. "So long, boy! You watch-a your step!"

The freight train gathered speed slowly, passed the roundhouse and crept along the embankment past the jungle. Campfires were still burning down among the trees. As he looked at the men huddled around them Vic felt glad to be on his way.

They entered the cut and the tracks kept converging at switches until there were only two sets ahead. They passed a "Yard Limit" sign and a few minutes later rounded a bend, and started across a great steel drawbridge that spanned the water of a canal.

Vic looked down; by the rain-diffused light thrown from lamps along a concrete wall, he saw a tugboat with a boom of logs behind it entering a lock. Beyond the lock the canal water reflected the lights burning on the city's surrounding hills. Then the bridge, the canal, and most of the lights were behind.

With the increasing speed, the rain blew in harder. Vic fastened all his buttons and crouched down in the forward corner of the car. Every now and then he popped up for a look around, but for a time he saw nothing but the dark waters to the left and a shadowy bank to the right. Then some lights appeared ahead, around a long, gentle curving of the Sound. The train sped through a small town, whistled for a crossing and, without changing speed, passed into darkness again. Blackie had certainly been mistaken when he said a freight train slowed down going through a town.

A mile or two ahead lights appeared on another point of land and soon Vic could see that they were from a ship moored at the end of a long pier. The train rounded the point and there was another dock with a ferry at it. This was the place!

Vic went over the side of the car and down the ladder with a death grip on the slippery grabirons. His feet found the stirrup at the bottom and he began looking for a place to jump.

The Malley was shrieking its authority at the crossing and the station lights were coming fast. The word "Edmonds" went by in a blur and Vic got ready to jump into the lighted area in front of the depot. But there was no slowdown here either, and he lost his nerve. Why, they must be doing fifty! he thought as the lights flashed by. He heard a "Ding, ding, ding!" and the train thundered over the crossing and on. There was nothing he could do now but stick with her. He climbed back up the ladder and dropped down into the car again.

Fifteen or twenty minutes later the speed diminished and the train leaned into a long curve. Vic heard the ringing of a crossing bell, looked out and saw lights go by and "Mukilteo" on a depot. They were going slowly enough now. Should he hop off and walk on back to Edmonds? As he started to go over the side he saw the lights of a city a few miles on ahead, and decided to wait and play it safe.

As they drew nearer the city, a green block signal changed to yellow and the train began to slow. A yard limit sign went by and switch lamps, glowing like huge red and green fireflies in the darkness, marked the splitting and spreading out of tracks.

Vic could just make out the name "Everett" on the dimly lighted railroad station, where a man was sitting behind a window wearing a green eyeshade and operating a telegraph key.

The train clattered over a bridge and there was a brief glimpse of wet streets, empty but for a garbage wagon rumbling along behind a team of glistening horses.

Without warning they were in the blackness of a tunnel where the atmosphere was suddenly hot and thick with engine smoke. Vic was afraid to breathe. He dropped down onto the floor of the car, held his breath until his head was spinning, and though he inhaled cautiously, he was almost strangled by the fumes. He was still gasping when they burst out of the tunnel. He coughed and tried to spit out the acrid taste, then he began to savor the sweetness of the cold, wet wind.

Beyond the tunnel, in another railroad yard, the train slowed and stopped.

Vic went down the ladder and dropped to the ground. Now he'd better start hoofing it back to Edmonds. It was going to be a long, cold, hungry walk—and the sooner he got started, the better. Nearby street lamps cast enough light into the yard so he could find his way back along the train. He was going past a boxcar when a fellow standing in the doorway said, "Do you know where we are?"

"I guess it's Everett."

"Slim!" It was Blackie. "What are you doing here? I thought you got off down the line."

"She was going too fast for me."

Blackie called back into the car. "Hey, Curly, Slim's out here!"

"Tell him to get in out of the rain."

Blackie reached a hand down. "Grab on and I'll heave you up."

"I think I'd better keep going, Blackie. I've got a long walk ahead of me."

"Aw, it'll keep. Come on, get in, we're just getting ready to split up those sandwiches the lady gave me yesterday."

Vic grabbed the offered hand and was hauled up into the boxcar. Blackie struck a match and they picked their way through the men sprawled out on the floor. It was the sandhouse scene all over again but without the stove or sand. Warmed by crowded bodies and protected from the wind, the boxcar was a lot more comfortable than the gondola had been.

Curly and Billie were sitting in the forward corner of the car. They moved over and made way for Vic and Blackie. Blackie's match went out and he struck another. The two sandwiches were divided, and when the second match burned out they sat eating in the darkness.

Outside, above the sound of rain and wind, they could hear the Malley backing down the adjoining track. As it passed, the headlight shining through the partly open boxcar door lighted up the interior and the sleeping men threw their arms across their eyes or turned their heads away. "What are they doing out there, anyway?" Vic asked.

"Setting out some empties, I guess," Curly said.

"I sure hope they don't set this one out," Billie said.

"Keep your fingers crossed. This is no night to be on the tops."

The engine came chuffing back, lighting up the car again as it passed. Curly said, "You must want to get home pretty bad to start out hiking in this stuff, Slim."

"I haven't got much choice."

"You'll catch pneumonia sure as anything."

"I've been out in worse weather than this and it never hurt me."

"How far do you have to go, twenty miles, thirty?"

"Something like that, I guess."

Curly frowned. "I was noticing those shoes of yours yesterday. They haven't even got ten miles left in them."

Vic looked down at his feet. There were holes through the bottoms of both shoes and the sole of one was pulling away from the upper.

"Why don't you ride on over to Wenatchee with us? At least you'll be in out of the weather. Maybe we can rustle you up another pair of shoes. We'll build a good big mulligan tomorrow and you can start back with a full belly."

"Maybe it will be done raining when you get back," Blackie said.

"That sounds like a good idea, but . . ."

"But what?" Billie asked.

Vic couldn't think of a response to Billie's question. The Malley answered for him. It coupled on with a crash, whistled, then jerked the train into motion.

"Are you staying with us?" Curly asked as they began to move.

The driving rain outside and the flapping shoes on his feet decided for him. "I guess I might as well," Vic answered and was surprised to feel so good about it.

A voice came out of the darkness at the other end of the car. "Hey, pipe down! We're tryin' to sleep."

Blackie struck another match and in its brief flaring they stretched out full length on the floor. Vic lay listening to the clicking rail joints and the rattlings and creakings of the freight train as it picked up speed. From the wheels below there came the steady, lulling, "Clickety-click, clickety-click, clickety-click, clickety-click . . ."

9

The top of Vic's head was slammed hard against the end of the boxcar as the train shuddered to a stop. He got up, picked his way to the door and looked out at the little station. "Gold Bar," he said, reading the sign on the depot.

"I've been here," Curly said. "This is where they pick up the helper. How's the weather outside?"

A sleepy-looking boy who had moved up to the door of the boxcar answered. "It ain't rainin'."

"That's good. I wonder what time it is."

"Almost mornin'," the boy said. "It's light enough to see the snow on the mountains."

"We must be up into the hills then."

Blackie sat up, moved nearer to the opening in the car, but immediately moved back. "Yeah, and it's colder'n an Eskimo's nose. I'm going to close the door."

One by one the other men stood up and stretched, then settled down where they had slept.

The Malley chuffed and the car jerked. "They're

breaking the train in two so they can put the helper in the middle," Curly said.

As the Malley got under way, another engine was heard going in the opposite direction down the next track. Its headlight shone through the cracks around the door as it went by.

The Malley hesitated for a moment, backed up, swerved, straightened. "Feels like they just switched us onto another track," Billie said.

Curly sat up. "Open up that door and let's see what's going on." The door was opened. "Hey, we're going into a storage yard!"

"Maybe they're picking up more empties," Blackie suggested.

The cut of cars stopped, the engine was uncoupled and taken away, leaving them there. "The heck they are, they just set us out!"

There was a rush for the door. In the half light of the breaking day, men were jumping out of the string of sidetracked boxcars and scurrying across the storage tracks to the main line. Vic followed his companions, tripping and stumbling over rails and ties in his haste. Curly looked up and down the train and swore. "I'll bet there isn't an empty left on this whole blasted drag."

"What do we do now?" Vic asked. He was starting to shiver again.

"Ride the tops. Come on!" Curly started up the grabirons, and the boys and Vic were right behind him. To left and right the cars swarmed with men going to the tops. The Malley coupled on and whistled, puffed, the slack jerked out of the drawbars, and the drag got under way.

For the first few miles the rails ran straight and level. The train quickly reached full speed and the sharp mountain air cut through Vic's damp clothing, chilling him to the bone. The wooden catwalk that ran down the center of the cartop was still soaking wet from last night's rain. But there was no place else to sit. Looking up and down the rocking train, Vic could see scores of other men huddled like him, with their backs hunched forward, collars up, and hands in pockets. Blackie moved closer to Vic and shivered. "Fun, isn't it?" The boy tried to grin.

"It'd be more fun inside, though."

"You'd miss all this scenery, then."

The scenery was something to look at. A river ran parallel to the roadbed, green water flowing deep and swift. Straight ahead saw-toothed crags were sharply outlined against a brightening skyline. Except for a line of dark clouds hanging over the lowlands behind them, the sky was clear. The sun was going to shine today—and it couldn't be too soon.

The Malley passed from sight around a bend, each car behind it disappearing in turn. The river turned here, too, and changed from glassy green to ragged white as the channel abruptly became steeper, shallower, and filled with boulders.

Beyond the curve the roadbed swung gently to the

right; soon the entire train was in sight, from Malley to caboose, winding up the grade at a pace little faster than a walk. Vic began counting the people on the cartops. He got to two hundred and twenty-three.

The foothills fell behind and the mountain walls closed in until the valley was a canyon. The river became a series of plunging waterfalls with foaming rapids in between. Other falls—thin, veily plumes of white—dangled from the clifftops. There were snow-fields on all the summits, and just the sight of them made Vic feel colder. "Boy," he said, "I've had about all of this I can take."

"Aw, this is nothin'," Billie said. "You want to try Tennessee Pass sometime."

"Where's that?"

"Colorado Rockies. She's ten thousand feet if she's an inch."

The train went through a town where logging locomotives sat rusting on a siding, crossed a turbulent stream and came out of the canyon into a mountain valley just as the sun broke over the peaks ahead. But the passing wind blew away any warmth the sun might have given.

When two rusty smokestacks appeared ahead and the train began to slow, Curly yelled, "Skykomish coming up! Keep your heads down, and watch out for the trolley wire!"

They passed the smokestacks which marked a shut-down lumber mill; the tracks began to split and a railroad yard appeared ahead. Above each pair of tracks hung an ominous copper wire from which the trolleys took the high-voltage current to power the electric locomotives on through the mountains. Vic ducked, needing no second warning to make him shy of it.

The town was cut in two by the yards. The road and part of the residences were to the right, the business district and the river to the left. Within the yards was a roundhouse and electrical substation.

As the freight train rolled into town, Blackie stretched his stiff muscles. "I wonder how long we'll be here?"

"Just long enough to take the Malley off and hook the motors on," Curly said. "About half an hour, as I remember."

"That's long enough to hit a couple of doors." Blackie started for the ladder. "Anybody coming with me?"

"You're wasting your time hustling here," Curly told him. "There's probably more boes on this drag than people in Skykomish."

"I'm going to give it a try, anyway." Blackie went down the grabirons and dropped off the moving train. Curly watched him cut across the tracks and disappear.

"If there's a stray sandwich in this town, that boy will find it."

The train stopped and the car Vic was on was directly in front of the depot. Inside, the agent was working at a typewriter. Outside, in a fenced-in garden between the platform and the main street, a Japanese was on his knees weeding flower beds. There was a drinking fountain bubbling at the corner of the garden.

"I'm thirsty," Vic said. "I wonder if they'd mind if I had a drink?"

"I don't see anybody there to stop you," Billie said.

They went down the ladder and over to the fountain, had a drink, and washed their hands and faces in the icy water. Then they walked up the platform to the far end of the depot and stood with their backs against the warm wall. The bright sun shone in their faces. "Boy, that sure feels good!" Vic said, unbuttoning his coat to let in the warmth.

"You better soak up all the sunshine you can, because the worst is yet to come." Curly pointed east to a sharp line cutting through the snow on a shaded slope farther up the valley where the railroad climbed higher into the mountains.

They watched the train crew meet on the depot platform and go across the street to a café in an old frame hotel building on a corner. Through a window they could see the men take seats at a counter where a waitress brought them cups of coffee.

Vic wondered what they were having for breakfast at home this morning. Oatmeal with brown sugar and cream on it or fried cornmeal mush flooded with melted butter and homemade syrup? It seemed an age that he'd been gone, and he didn't even know what day it was.

From down the street, a block or so past the café, a school bell began to ring and children started going by with books and lunches in their hands.

Curly walked around the corner of the depot and looked down the street. "I wonder how Blackie's making out?"

"He's probably sittin' with his feet under somebody's breakfast table right this minute," Billie said.

"I don't doubt that a bit. That boy will ride the varnish yet."

Billie turned around so that his back was to the sun and his face toward the depot. "Well, look who's been here." He pointed to some letters that had been cut deeply and neatly into the wood of the depot, "TEX K.T."

"That's his mark, all right," Curly said, "the *real* Tex."

"He sure gets around. I've seen that carved or painted on fences and buildings from one end of the country to the other."

"Yeah, but a lot of them are cut by phonies, Billie. It's getting so every kid with a jackknife or a piece of chalk is putting 'TEX K.T.' on everything." Curly ran a finger along the letters on the depot wall. "But old Tex himself did this."

"What does the 'K.T.' mean, anyway?" Vic asked.

"King of Tramps."

"Is he the King of Tramps?"

"He seems to think so," Curly said. "But I'm not a tramp, so I wouldn't know."

"What do you mean?" Vic looked surprised. "Aren't tramps and hobos all the same thing?"

"I should say not!"

"What's the difference?"

"A hobo has self-respect and a tramp doesn't."

"How about a bum?"

"A bum is just no good at all."

"How do you tell them apart?"

"You'll know 'em when you see 'em."

Vic nodded. "I met a bum back in Seattle." He was thinking of George Brown.

The train crew finished breakfast and came back across the street. They split up in front of the depot and the three head-end men went up the tracks, the rear brakeman to the crossing. The conductor went inside and came out minutes later with the station agent. He was a heavy-shouldered man with bushy hair and walked as though he might have worn a wooden leg. They stood in the sunlight talking and joking, looking now and then toward the front of the train. Finally the long, drawn-out blast of an air whistle echoed down the valley. The semaphore ahead was green.

"Blackie better be gettin' back," Billie said. He looked up and down the street behind the depot.

"That whistle will bring him running," Curly said.

The conductor took a newspaper from his pocket and signaled with it toward the rear section of the train down beyond the crossing. With dynamos humming, the motor began creeping forward. Its bell was ringing and as it blew the crossing whistle the brakeman stepped out into the street to flag oncoming traffic.

Billie looked about uneasily. "I wish Blackie would come."

The motor closed the gap, slowed to almost stopping, and coupled onto the forward section of the train so gently that it hardly moved the end boxcar. The agent limped back into the depot and came out again with some green papers in his hand. He gave them to the conductor. "Here's your orders, Nap. Get out of town!"

"As soon as I get my passengers on." The conductor grinned and called, "All aboard!" and the hobos who'd been standing around began going to the tops. The train began to move.

Curly reached for the grabirons. "Come on, boys, we better get on while we can." He went up the ladder, and Vic followed him.

"What about Blackie?" Billie said, looking back over his shoulder.

"He can take care of himself!" Curly called down from the top of the boxcar. "Come on, get on!"

Billie caught the grabirons and scrambled to the top of the car and looked around. "There he comes now!" Blackie was racing down a side street from the direction of the river. He had a brown paper sack in his hand.

Powered by the double set of electric motors, the train was picking up speed fast. "Do you think he'll make it?" Vic asked.

"If he doesn't, we'll wait for him in Wenatchee," Curly said.

Blackie sprinted across the street toward the depot. He disappeared between the far end of the building and the flower garden. Coming into view again, he ran along the platform, parallel to the accelerating freight train.

"He'll never make it!" Billie said and started over the side of the car.

"Where you going?" Curly yelled at him.

"I'm goin' to drop off and lay over with him."

Vic saw Blackie reach for the grabirons, saw the sack slip from his hand, saw him grab for it, saw him trip and stumble into the narrow space between the platform and the tracks. The sack burst and bits of sandwiches scattered in front of the depot.

"He went under!" Billie yelled as he went down the ladder.

Cursing savagely, Curly went over the side and dropped off the train.

Vic saw the station agent run into the depot. Then the arm of the semaphore ahead dropped and the light turned red. With a hiss of air and grinding brake shoes, the train slowed and came to a halt. Vic jumped off and ran back to the station.

All along the train men were getting off, hurrying to join the group gathered around a boxcar in front of the depot. Others stood on the tops looking down. Trembling and out of breath, Vic hesitated at the edge of the crowd. He could see nothing but the backs of the heads and shoulders of several people standing down between the rails and the platform. He could see Curly's shiny bald head and the station agent's bushy one. Then the agent stepped back up onto the platform, turned and limped heavily through the crowd. Looking toward the flower beds he called, "George, go over to the town hall and tell Carl to bring the box." The Japanese nodded and put down his trowel.

The crowd was silent but for an occasional low-voiced comment. "Boy, what a way to get it!"

"He never knew what happened."

"I saw him go under and he didn't make a sound."

"Yes, sir, a real quick trip to the Big Rock Candy Mountain."

A boy in a grimy-gray sweat shirt was picking up the bits of scattered sandwiches and putting them into his pocket.

An old truck came rattling up the street and stopped at the rear of the platform. The gardener got out, followed by the driver, a tall, lean man with a badge pinned to his shirt and a holstered revolver on his belt.

They unloaded an oblong metal box, lettered on the top, "King County Coroner, Seattle, Washington." The crowd parted for them to go through; when they set the box down on the edge of the platform it resounded like a drum. Vic heard the squeak of unoiled hinges as the lid was opened. Curly and the conductor lifted something from the roadbed and lowered it gently into the box.

"I wish I had those shoes. They're just about my size," someone said.

"Go get 'em. He won't need 'em any more."

"No, thanks."

Curley and Billie disappeared under the boxcar. "They're going back after the rest of him," someone murmured. One man began to vomit.

Vic turned and walked away, a hand to his eyes to hide his tears. He heard a lid slam shut and the snapping of a lock. There was a rumbling on the platform and he turned to see the station agent coming along, pulling a four-wheeled hand truck. Half a dozen men hoisted the box onto the truck and pulled it into the baggage room.

The station agent took out some keys and unlocked a rest room door. "You fellows better go in and wash up." He looked at Curly and Billie. They went inside and the conductor and the officer followed them.

The agent spoke to the gardener. "Get your hose out, George."

The officer came out of the rest room drying his hands on a paper towel. "Do you want to take down the information for me, Jim?"

"Sure, Carl. Bring them into the depot."

The officer addressed the men standing around the platform. "Is there anybody here who knew the boy?"

"We were traveling with him," Curly said. His voice was husky.

"Come on inside, will you? We have to get some information for the coroner."

Vic followed them into the office. The agent put a sheet of paper into a typewriter and the officer said, "What was his name?"

Curly shrugged. "I don't know his real name."

"We called him Blackie," Billie said. His voice was so low it could scarcely be heard.

The agent typed a few words.

"Do you know where he was from?"

They shook their heads. "I met him last summer in Detroit," Billie said, "but he never said where his folks lived."

"How old was he?"

Billie turned to Curly. "When was it we had that birthday party for him?"

"We were in Fresno—three weeks ago, wasn't it?"

"Yeah, about that. He was fifteen then."

The agent frowned, blinked his eyes, and tapped the keys.

"Religion?"

They shook their heads.

"How about you, Slim, do you know anything about him?"

Vic shook his head. "I only met him yesterday."

The officer turned to the agent. "What have you got there, Jim?"

The man read from what he had typed. "Transient, fifteen years old; name and address unknown; nickname, 'Blackie'; killed while attempting to board moving Train No. 402 at Skykomish, Washington, at —" He glanced up at the clock on the wall. "That would have been about ten minutes ago." He struck the typewriter keys. "—at 9:05 A.M. this date."

"I guess that'll have to do it."

The agent folded the paper and handed it to the officer.

The conductor, who'd been standing by, said, "Can we leave now?"

The agent tapped a telegraph key, listened to the clicking answer, and nodded. "Any time, Nap."

"Say, Mister," Billie said, "what happens to him now?"

"He'll go to Seattle in a baggage coach this afternoon. The coroner will see that he gets a decent burial."

"Thanks, Mister."

As they came out into the sunlight the gardener was washing down the tracks in front of the depot with a high-pressure water hose.

Through a window they saw the agent push a lever over his desk. Far up the track the semaphore arm returned to an upright position and the light changed from red to green. The conductor waved his paper and the motor whistled. The drawbars clattered down the line and the train began to move.

Curly and the boys walked across the platform.

Through the open door of the baggage room they could see the metal box resting on the hand truck in the shadows. Billie reached for the grabirons. Halfway up the ladder he hesitated and waved a hand toward the receding depot. As he followed to the tops, Vic heard him say, "Blackie's goin' to ride the varnish after all."

10

The breeze that passed over the cartops was warm. It carried the fragrance from the forests on the slopes, and the wild flowers in the meadows. The brilliant sunlight brought out the details of the constantly changing mountain landscape, but the two boys and the man sitting on the catwalk seemed unaware of their surroundings.

Curly had been talking incessantly ever since the train had left Skykomish. Billie and Vic sat staring ahead without answering.

"I can't wait till we get to a jungle so I can cut these blasted whiskers off." Curly scratched at the brown and gray stubble that had sprouted from his weathered face. "What do you say we have a smoke?" He took out his tobacco and papers and rolled a cigarette, offered it to Billie but the boy ignored it. "All right, then I'll smoke the blasted thing myself."

They climbed steadily through a gorge with a green-white river far below. At its narrowest point the gorge was spanned by a tall steel bridge. Vic clutched the catwalk as the train crept across, and closed his eyes to shut out the dizzy drop below. On the other side of the bridge they were drawn into the shadow of the mountain and it was cold again. As they climbed higher and higher, patches of snow began to appear in the deeper gulches, then they saw some here and there along the tracks, and soon it was all around them. The waterfalls tumbling down the precipices were laced with blue icicles, and the ditches and ponds along the right-of-way were frozen over. Vic shivered and buttoned his mackinaw.

The grade lessened perceptibly and the train began to pick up speed. "Here comes the big hole!" Curly yelled.

Straight ahead, in the center of a concrete abutment set into the foot of a mountain, was the black, inverted U of a tunnel portal, with a cloud of mist wafting from it. Vic read a sign by the tracks just before his car was drawn through the mist. "Cascade Tunnel, longest tunnel in the Western Hemisphere. 7.8 miles."

It had been cold enough outside, but the tunnel was like an icebox. The concrete walls exuded a damp chill and echoed back the noises of the freight train, until they were magnified into a roar. His ears hurt and Vic yelled back in anger, but couldn't hear his voice at all. And he couldn't see either. He felt lost in a world of wind and roaring noises.

After a few minutes his eyes began adjusting to the darkness and he saw an eerie line of blue lights ahead. Then he detected other lights besides the spooky strings of bulbs. Farther up the tunnel was the leading motor's headlight, and toward the rear the helper's yellow eye sent rays out over the tops. Now he could see the silhouettes of men crouched low, wary of the trolley wire. Vic's car flashed by a bright green block signal mounted on the side of the tunnel and he caught a fleeting glimpse of Billie and Curly. Curly had an arm around Billie's shoulders.

As suddenly as they had entered it they came out of the tunnel. One instant they were enduring bitter cold and thundering darkness; the next, they were blinking in the warm sunlight.

The deafness soon wore off, and before long the clicking of the wheels and whistle of the wind were audible again. It was a pleasant dry wind, lacking the salty tang of the sea and beach and the musty odor of damp forestlands on the ocean side of the Cascades. Everything here seemed different to Vic. He saw his first pine forests and blue elderberry bushes and cottonwoods. He watched eagerly to see what new sight the next curve might bring into view.

Soon towns appeared along the tracks—Merritt, Winton, Chiwaukum. They amounted to little more than the signs on the depots.

The mountains became lower, the valleys broader. Farmhouses and fields appeared, with sheep-filled pastures and white-faced cattle. At Chumstick, men on horseback watched the train go by.

Somewhere along the line they lost the vivacious little stream that had been accompanying them, but it reappeared at Leavenworth, deep and green, and flowing sedately from a canyon.

The canyon marked the ending of the mountains. From there on the river wound leisurely down a pleasant valley where orchards climbed surrounding foothills.

Vic was so struck by the beauty of the region that for a time he forgot what had happened at Skykomish. The sparkling river, the green hillsides, the precisely laid-out orchards, and the neat towns—Dryden, Cashmere, Monitor—were set against a backdrop of deep blue sky where cottony thunderheads stood tall above a plateau to the east. A long freight train was standing on a siding near Monitor, with hobos in every car. "There's your westbound drag, Slim!" Curly yelled as they went by.

The valley ended abruptly and the stream's greenness was swallowed by the muddy current of a great river flowing down from the north along the foot of the plateau. "There's the Columbia!" Curly yelled.

In another minute the rails made a turn and a fair-sized city appeared on the right-hand bank of the Columbia. A big signboard bore the invitation, "Welcome to Wenatchee, Apple Capital of the World!"

"I wonder if that welcome is for us, too," Billie said. The train slowed, passed between the business district and a row of big cold-storage fruit warehouses, went under a highway bridge, and came to a stop in a railroad yard.

"End of the line!" a trainman called, and the hobos began unloading.

The jungle was in a strip of vacant land between the tracks and the river, an old dumping ground for cast-off refuse of the railroad. A few low bushes and outcroppings of brown rock were the only natural shelter. But discarded ties had been piled up for windbreaks, and there were many little shacks made of sticks and cardboard.

At the foot of the embankment there was a water faucet. A few boilin'-up cans were hung upside down on stakes driven into the ground nearby, and there were men and campfires everywhere. "Boy, look at that mob!" Billie said.

"They must be here to work in the orchards," Curly said. "It's just about thinning and spraying time, I guess."

The information didn't cheer up Billie. "I don't know why they're here but somethin' tells me pickin's are gonna be tough in this town."

"I wonder when I'll be able to catch a ride back?" Vic said.

"Let's worry about that after we get something under our belts," Curly said, reaching for a boilin'-up can. "You lads better get cleaned up and start hustling, because this new crowd that just hit town is going to give you some real competition. I'll get the fire going and have things all set up for a mulligan when you get back."

So, when they'd washed and tidied up the best they could, Vic and Billie started hiking toward town along the railroad tracks. Ahead, they saw a group of Negroes coming toward them. "They've all got their pockets full of somethin'," Billie said.

When they met, Billie stopped. "How's pickin's, fellas?"

"Pickin's are fine if you like apples," one of them answered. He took one from a bulging pocket and tossed it to Billie. Someone else gave one to Vic. "We been in this town a week and ain't seen nothin' *but* apples."

They all shook their heads and one of the older men said, "The police won't even let you out of the yards."

"Maybe so, but we'll give it a try, anyway."

They walked on up the railroad tracks and looked around. "If there's cops up ahead to keep us out of town we'd better slip in behind them. C'mon, let's get up there on that street. Now, remember, Slim," Billie said as they cut across a brushy hillside and came out on a paved roadway, "if we get stopped we're just a couple of apple-knockers comin' in to do a little shoppin'. I'm gonna get some pants and you need new shoes."

"Boy, I *do* need 'em, too. The sole of this left one is starting to flap."

"We'll look for a piece of string to tie around it. That'll get you sympathy when we start hittin' the back doors." He stopped and picked up a cigarette butt. "Keep your eye peeled for snipes, too."

"Why? I don't smoke."

"I know. But if you got some smokin' in your pocket, you can always get in on a mulligan."

After a ten-minute walk they saw a big white house ahead. "That's as good a place as any to start, even if it has got fresh paint on it," Billie said. But at the driveway they saw the sign, "NO HANDOUTS!" And at the next house, "KEEP GOING, BUM!" and at the next, "KEEP OUT, THIS MEANS YOU!"

"You'd think we'd be far enough from the yards by now so that we wouldn't be seeing any more of those signs," Vic said.

"When boes are in hungry country they roam for miles. That's what Curly told me, and he knows. These places look just too prosperous for handouts, anyway. The more people got, the stingier they are. Let's swing straight on into town. We'll starve to death out in these orchards."

When they reached the residential district they found a frayed piece of rope lying by the wayside and sat down while Vic tied it around his shoe. They rested for a while and had a drink of water from an irrigation ditch.

Then Billie said, "You take this street and I'll work

the next one over, Slim. I'll meet you in front of that brick church down there in about an hour. And keep that bum shoe out where they can see it."

Hungry as he was, Vic found it was just as hard to beg here as it had been in Seattle. He passed up several houses before getting up the nerve to turn in at one. When he finally started up the walk a woman looked out the window and shook her head, waving to him to go away. He kept on going.

Farther down the block he saw a thin little woman struggling to push a lawnmower through a crop of tall grass. "Could I help you, lady?"

"Thank you." She sat down on the front steps and directed the work of mowing and raking and where to dump the cuttings. When the front lawn was done she asked him to do the back; then she inspected the entire yard and had him go over some places he had missed. She had him edge the walks and weed the flower beds, and then showed him where to put the tools away. When everything was done she said, "You are very kind," and went inside and closed the door behind her. Vic looked after her in outrage. She hadn't even offered him a glass of water.

It was late in the afternoon and he went directly to the church, which was on the shady side of the street. Billie was already there and Vic sat down beside him on the cool stone steps. He was hot, tired, hungry and discouraged. "Where you been all this time?" Billie asked. Vic told him.

"That was your own fault, Slim. She didn't promise you nothin'. You should have told her you'd cut the grass for a bite to eat."

Vic nodded.

"You're gettin' educated. You'll know better next time."

"Well, how'd you make out?"

Billie spread his empty hands. "I never heard so many hard luck stories in my life. If I don't eat pretty soon I'm gonna do somethin' desperate."

"I sure wish Blackie was here. Maybe he could . . ."

"Well, he ain't!" Billie's words were sharp and final.

Vic contemplated his tied-on shoe sole for a time. "Want to go get some of those apples?"

"You can't fill up on fruit." Billie looked around, lowered his voice. "If we can just hold out till dark we can go lookin' for unlocked doors."

"What do you mean?"

Billie's face was grim. "If they won't give us any handouts in this town, we'll take it away from 'em."

Vic shook his head. "Count me out, Billie."

"We'll find a house with no lights on; you'll keep watch and I'll go in and take a look around."

"Nope. I don't want any part of it." Vic got up and hobbled off, his foot hurting from the rope around his shoe.

Billie got up and followed. "Okay, okay, we won't then." They walked along in silence for a time. "You've still got that change, haven't you, Slim?"

He felt in his pockets and nodded.

"How much you got?"

"About eighty cents."

"That's enough to keep us honest for a day or so. Let's pick up a can of beans or somethin'."

"All right, let's." At a small grocery store a couple of blocks away they bought two large cans of pork and beans for a quarter, and the proprietor let them have two loaves of stale bread for a dime. Vic was craving sweets and spent another nickel for a chocolate bar.

He broke it into thirds and when they'd eaten their portions, Billie said, "Let's split that other piece, too."

"Shouldn't I save that for Curly?"

"What he don't know won't hurt him." They divided Curly's piece and ate it.

The street they were on led downhill through the business district and ended at the railroad tracks. They crossed over to one of the cold-storage warehouses and helped themselves to the boxes of cull apples on the loading platform. Then they went back to the jungle.

There they found Curly sitting on a chunk of wood tending a boilin'-up can steaming over a small fire. Vic hardly recognized him. He had washed and shaved and combed his hair and was wearing only his shoes and trousers. His underclothes and socks and shirt had been laundered and were hanging on nearby bushes drying in the sun. "How's pickings?" he asked.

"We got lots of apples." Billie tossed one to Curly.

"What's in the sack, Slim, more apples?"

"Pork and beans and bread."

"Good boy! What did you do, swipe it?"

"No. I had some change in my pocket."

Vic cut the top out of one of the cans with his knife and they made sandwiches of pork and beans between thick slabs of hard, dry bread. "Boy, that was good," Billie said when the loaf was gone and the can was empty. "Shall we open the other one?"

"No," Curly said, "we'd better fill up on apples. That other can of beans and the rest of the bread is going to look mighty good later on. It's a long old haul from here to Spokane."

"We're pulling out tonight?"

"Might as well. Things can't be any worse over there."

Vic looked out at the Columbia, running bankful and murky at springtime flood stage. It carried trees and floating debris. A small footbridge drifted by, and as he watched it, Vic wondered where it had come from. The footbridge vanished around a bend in the river, and the tracks of the railroad disappeared there, too. "I wonder what it's like around that bend," he said, more to himself than anybody else.

"Slim, you've got an itchy foot," Curly said.

Vic looked beyond the river toward the plateau where the black thunderheads were standing. And what lay over there? "I guess you're right, Curly."

"Then why are you going back home? Why don't you string along with us?"

"I don't like being hungry."

"It's not always this way. We're just having a run of bad luck."

Vic didn't reply. He was thinking of Blackie.

Billie washed his clothes in the boilin'-up can and hung them on the bushes to dry; when fresh water had been heated, Vic did some laundry, too. Afterwards he had a bath. There was no soap or towel but the cold water certainly made him feel better.

When Curly's clothes had dried he dressed and went up into the yards to find out about train schedules. "We can get out of here about nine o'clock," he told them when he returned.

At sunset the air grew chilly. Their clothes were still a bit damp, but Vic and Billie hurried into them and stood close to the fire to finish drying out.

As darkness settled over the jungle, the fires brightened and men gathered close around them for warmth and companionship. Several late-comers strolled by with wood and were accepted into the circle.

Everything that needed to be said was soon said and they stared into the fire, each one occupied with his own thoughts . . . each one alone, in a world of lean and silent men.

The Negroes around the adjoining fire were just as lean, their clothes as tattered and their shoes as worn, but they were not a silent group. They joked and laughed and sang.

The evening waned, the night deepened, and the moon rising full and bright cast its reflection on the river. In the yards, switchmen's lanterns gleamed like diamonds among the emeralds and rubies of the green and red switch lamps. A big road engine backed out of the roundhouse and stopped at a waterspout. When the tank was filled, it moved up to take on oil.

"Looks like she's getting ready to roll," Curly said. "Maybe we'd better eat now. Come on." Curly got up and left the fire, and Vic and Billie followed. They went off by themselves and opened the other can of beans, sliced the remaining loaf of bread, and had more pork-and-bean sandwiches. They polished off the apples. "All right, Billie, let's go see if our berths are ready."

"I'll come along and see you off," Vic said.

"Then you're still set on headin' back west?" Billie asked.

Vic nodded.

The rear half of the train was sealed refrigerator cars, with water dripping from the ice compartments and smelling fragrantly of apples. Flatcars came next, piled with pitchy, aromatic timbers, and gondolas full of stone. The boxcars were at the head.

"I'm glad we found these," Curly said. "It's going to be wet tonight." The clouds had spread out, hiding the moon and covering more than half the sky. As he spoke there was a flash of lightning just beyond the river, a crash of thunder, and big raindrops began pelting down.

"Here she comes!" Curly boosted Billie up into the boxcar and in turn was given a hand up. "You'd better get in, Slim, if you don't want to get drowned." They hauled Vic up.

The cloudburst brought the hobos running from the jungle. Vic watched them, silhouetted against the lightning flashes, as they threw their packs and bedrolls through the door. They were still climbing in when the engine whistled and the train jerked into motion.

"Hey!" Vic yelled. "I want to get off!"

"We'll be halfway to Rock Island by the time you get to the door," Curly said. "You might as well come along with us, Slim. At least you'll be out of the rain."

Vic was easily persuaded.

Billie struck a match and they found a place on the floor to stretch out. The train picked up speed and went rolling down the banks of the dark Columbia, accompanied by the driving rain and an occasional thunderclap.

11

Vic sat up drowsily. The train had stopped and men were stumbling around in the darkness. "What's up?"

"They just sidetracked us again!"

Vic got up stiffly from the splintery floor, stepped on someone's foot and was cursed at. He excused himself. "Where are we?"

A strange voice answered. "Ephrata."

He heard other voices. "She's sure comin' down out there."

"Get a move on, fella, get a move on!"

As he shuffled along with the others toward the dimly outlined door, Vic heard Billie call, "Where are you, Curly?"

"Right here. You coming, Slim?"

"I'm right behind you."

They stood at the door a moment, then jumped blindly out into the driving rain and landed in the cinders. In the distance there was an occasional flash of lightning, followed by the grumble of thunder. The engine was backing down the main line, headlight pointing up the glistening rails ahead. The only other light was cast by the red and green lenses of a switch lantern. Everyone was attracted to it and by its feeble glow men were climbing up to the tops. Someone said, "I ain't gonna like this ride at all."

"Then get out of the way and let a man by that's leavin'."

The engine coupled on again, the air brakes hissed, the whistle blew.

"Hey, you guys, get aboard! We ain't got all night!" And then a hundred men were all trying to get back on at once.

The engine chuffed, the couplers jarred, the train began to move. Through the sheets of rain Vic saw Billie going up a ladder, outlined in the cherry-colored light from the red side of the lantern. He saw Curly reach for the grabirons and start climbing. "Come on, Slim!"

The car vanished in the darkness. Men kept crowding in ahead of him, and by the time Vic got to the tie ends the cars were beginning to blur. He made a grab, his hands slipped on the wet iron and he lost his hold. He braced himself and was about to make another desperate try when a voice behind him said, "She's goin' mighty fast, boy. Better wait over for the next one."

The train *was* going mighty fast. He stepped back

beside the figure standing on the green side of the switch lantern and watched the rest of the cars go by—the timber flats, the gondolas and tanks and refrigerators. He had one last sniff of apples before the rain drove the odor into the ground. The caboose whizzed past, yellow light shining from its windows, and the two red tail lamps disappeared.

Vic stood close against the side of the depot, sheltered from the rain by an overhanging eave, and looked around. The drizzle seemed lighter, and in the distance the sky was clear in patches and the moon and stars were shining through. He looked the other way, toward the town. Except for street lights shining at the intersections, everything was dark.

He crossed the street and started up the sidewalk. At the end of the block a powerful flashlight was shone into his face and he almost bumped into a man coming around the corner. The turned-down brim of his hat dripped and his raincoat glistened. A no-monkey-business voice said, "Stop right there!"

Vic stopped. "Who are . . ."

"The town marshal. Where did you come from?"

"I got stranded here by a freight train. I was just going to walk around and keep warm till another freight came along."

"They don't stop here very often, sometimes only once a week."

"Then maybe I can hitchhike out of here in the morning."

"Maybe, but I can't let you wander around the

town all night. Come along to the courthouse and I'll find you a place to sleep." As they walked down the street the marshal said, "What are you doing? Just bumming around?"

"I'm looking for a job."

"What can you do?"

"Well, I grew up on a farm and I've worked in the woods."

The marshal didn't comment, but led the way down some steps and into the basement of the courthouse. At the end of a hall they stopped in front of a barred door.

"What's this," Vic asked, "the jail?"

The marshal nodded and took some keys from his pocket.

"But I haven't done anything wrong."

"No." He unlocked the door and it swung open. "And as long as you're in here you won't, either."

The marshal flicked on a switch, lighting up a steel-barred cage set in the center of the cement-walled room. The cage was divided into cells; the door of one was closed, all the others stood open.

Bedsprings creaked in the locked cell and a head raised up. "Bringing us company, Marshal?"

"It's just a young fellow with no place to sleep, Eddie." He indicated the cell farthest from the occupied one and Vic stepped inside. It had top and bottom bunks, a wash bowl and a toilet. Stacks of old *Western Story* and *Argosy* magazines were piled in a corner.

"You sure look like something the cat dragged in," the marshal said. "Don't you even have a comb?"

"Someone stole all my stuff a couple of nights ago."

The marshal left the jail and returned with a toothbrush and a comb, a bar of soap and a towel stamped "Property of Grant County." He also brought a brown envelope. "I'll have to ask you to empty your pockets."

He wrote Vic's name and listed his possessions on the face of the envelope: "One mouth organ, one pocketknife, forty cents." He put them in the envelope and sealed it. "The girl in the office will give this back to you in the morning." He left the cell open but locked the outer door. "Have a good sleep." Then he switched off the light.

"Thanks a lot, Marshal."

A voice from the locked cell muttered, "Thanks for being put in jail—that's a good one."

Vic hung his damp clothes over the top bunk to dry. He washed, brushed his teeth and combed his hair. He climbed into the lower bunk. The mattress was hard, the springs were stiff and the blankets rough and musty-smelling, but it was the first bed he'd been in since leaving home and it sure felt good. Outside, the rain was spattering on the sidewalks and gurgling down the gutters. Being in jail wasn't so bad —as long as you knew you'd be let out in the morning.

Somewhere overhead a clock struck twice. Vic fell asleep.

He was awakened by the sound of voices and footsteps. It took a few minutes to remember where he was. Through a barred window set high in the basement wall he could see the legs of people walking past the courthouse. From the other end of the cage he heard the rattle of eating utensils and he could smell the aroma of coffee. He sat up on the edge of the bunk, stretched and began to dress. Someone in the occupied cell called out, "Hey, fella, are you awake?"

Vic yawned. "Yep."

"Come on down here and let's see what you look like."

Vic stepped out into the aisle and went to the locked cell. There were two young men inside. They were sitting on the lower bunk eating from trays set on a wooden bench. There was a coffee pot between them.

"Hello," Vic said, eying the food.

"Boy, are you skinny!" one of the prisoners said. "I'll bet you have to stand twice in one place to cast a shadow."

"Oh, knock it off, Eddie," the other said. "Did Joe leave a tray for you?"

"I didn't see any."

"I guess they only feed the prisoners. Hungry?"

"I sure am."

"You look like you got a tapeworm," Eddie told him.

"Why don't you shut up?" the other prisoner said. He took a piece of toast from his tray, spread jam on it and held it through the bars. "Here, I've got more than I can eat."

Vic took the toast. "Thanks."

Eddie picked up the coffee pot, filled a cup. "Here's something to wash it down with." He passed the cup through the bars.

"Do you like mush?" the other said.

"You bet."

"You can have mine. I don't like the stuff."

"Why don't you go get that bench over there? You can sit on one end and eat off the other."

Vic brought the bench, and a bowl of mush, a can of milk, and a sugar bowl were handed out to him.

"You can have mine, too," Eddie said. "Where did you come from?"

"Off a freight train."

"Why did you stop in this burg? There's nothing here."

"They set out the car I was in and the train got going too fast before I had a chance to get on again."

"Boy, just give me the chance," Eddie said. "I'll bet I'd get aboard." He shoved another piece of toast through the bars.

Vic took the toast and wiped the last of the mush and milk from the bowl with it. "How long have you two been in here?"

"Oh, about a month." The prisoner picked up the coffee pot. "Give me your cup, Slim."

"We're in for bank robbery," Eddie volunteered.

His cellmate glowered at him. "You talk too much. That's what got us in here." He emptied the coffee pot into Vic's cup. "What are you gonna do when you leave here?"

"If I can't find a job I guess I'll have to go back home."

Eddie put his plate against the bars. "Let me scrape these scrambled eggs into that bowl."

"Thanks." When Vic had eaten the eggs, he said, "How long will you have to stay here?"

"We haven't had a trial yet, but our lawyer says we'll be lucky if he can get us off with a five-to-ten."

"Five-to-ten?"

"Five to ten years in Walla Walla."

"The state penitentiary! Wow!"

"These yokels don't like people foolin' with their money box," Eddie said.

Footsteps echoed down the outer hall and the marshal appeared at the jail door. Another man was with him. "Good morning, Martin, did you have a good sleep?"

"Yes, sir. Thank you."

"Last night you said you wanted a job. Did you mean it?"

"Yes, sir."

The marshal introduced the man with him. "This is Mr. Albrecht. He's looking for a ranch hand. Walter, this is Vic Martin, the lad I was telling you about."

Mr. Albrecht had a scraggly gray mustache and was wearing a battered, dusty hat. He looked about sixty and would have been of average height had he not been so stoop-shouldered. There were deep lines in his weathered face and around his pale blue eyes. Even in the dimness of the jail corridor he squinted.

144

He stood with the thumbs of gnarled, work-worn hands hooked into the suspender straps of his patched bib overalls. He spoke with a German accent. "You grow up on a farm, yah?"

"Yes, sir."

"You have horses on that farm?"

"No, but I drove a team in the woods and the berry fields."

"You worked in fruit, eh?"

"Loganberries and a little in the apples."

"Can you drive a Ford?"

"Sure."

Mr. Albrecht turned to the marshal. "Yah, I think I take him." He spoke as though he was buying a head of cattle.

The marshal unlocked the door. "All right, get your things."

Vic hesitated. "What's the pay?"

"I give you twenty dollars a month and room and board."

"I'll take it," Vic said before the man could change his mind. Boy, that was a fortune. He went back to the cell for his coat.

"You can keep that comb and soap and toothbrush," the marshal called after him. "Just leave us the towel."

Vic put on his coat, pocketed the toilet articles, then went to the occupied cell. "Thanks for the chow, boys, and lots of luck."

"We'll need it," Eddie said. "Don't work too hard."

In the office a girl returned his possessions. "Drop in

and see us any time," the marshal said. "I'd like to know how you're making out."

"I will, and thanks again for everything." They shook hands.

"Come," Mr. Albrecht said. "We go now."

A clock was just striking nine as they went out the door and into the morning sunshine. The rancher led the way to an old green Model-T truck parked at the curb. Vic had seen many like it at home, vehicles rebuilt from parts scavenged in junk yards or stripped from broken-down flivvers abandoned by the roadside. The squared-off brass radiator was from a 1914 model, the low-roofed open cab was homemade, the windshield was cracked, and the hood was held on with baling wire. The narrow, thirty-by-three clincher-rim tires were worn smooth. Mr Albrecht slid in under the steering wheel, flipped on the ignition switch, and a coil began to buzz. "Give her a twist!"

"I will when you retard that spark!" Vic said. He didn't want a broken arm.

The driver pushed the spark lever up and the gas down. Vic took hold of the crank and got ready to jump out of the way if he had to. You never could tell about these old Fords. He gave the crank a spin, the motor spat and began to chug, and the truck started to roll forward. He jumped aside and as it went by stepped onto the running board and swung into the cab. "Your brake band's shot!" he yelled over the noise.

Mr. Albrecht nodded and steered away from the

curb. A couple of blocks down the street he stopped in front of a grocery store. They got out and he took off the sacks that covered two cases of eggs.

"You bring them in."

Vic carried the cases into the store and put them in a cooler. The eggs were sold in exchange for coffee, a pound of tobacco, and a sack of flour. The rancher held a hand out for his change and the grocer said, "Why don't we put the rest of it on your bill, Walter?"

"I got to have cash to buy my spray."

The merchant shrugged and counted out several dollar bills and some change. Mr. Albrecht pocketed it and picked up the tobacco and coffee. "You bring the flour." Vic carried the sack to the truck.

"Now we go get the spray." Vic cranked up and they drove to a feed and implement house down by the tracks. "You wait out here," the rancher said.

Vic leaned against the side of the truck and glanced around. This was his first chance to have a good look at the town. It was neat looking with tree-lined streets, like an oasis set down in a barren countryside. Across the tracks there were grain elevators, a stockyard, and some oil tanks. Behind it was a low, brush-covered hill that blocked out everything that might lie beyond. A road crossed the tracks beyond the depot and angled up the side of the hill.

Things seemed different in the daylight than they had in the stormy early morning hours. The only sign left of the rain was a few puddles in the road, and they were drying rapidly. Down past the depot was the switch where he'd last seen Billie and Curly, going up the side of a boxcar. He wondered if he would ever see them again.

From inside the warehouse there came the sound of rising voices and Vic heard a man say, "That's final, Walter, no pay, no spray!"

"I'll pay you after the harvest."

"You haven't paid me for last year's spray yet!"

"If the codling moth gets into my trees, you'll *never* get it!"

"All right, all right, you win. You can have the spray but this is the last time, Walter, codling moth or no codling moth."

A few minutes later a big man in striped overalls wheeled a hand truck out the door and across the loading platform. He set down some heavy cans and Vic transferred them to the bed of the truck. When they were tied in place, Mr. Albrecht said, "All right, we go now."

They drove away from the implement house, around the block, and stopped in front of a pool hall. There was a sign in the window, "WE HAVE BEER!" The rancher shut the engine off. "I want to try some of that new beer. You wait here."

Vic remained in the truck. Through the pool hall window he could see his employer gulp down a glass of beer and buy another.

After a half hour's waiting Vic began to get restless. The clock struck ten; he got out and walked up the block and back to stretch his legs. When he returned, Mr. Albrecht was still sitting at the counter. There were two men with him now, one on either side. They all had full glasses before them.

Vic walked around some more, bought a candy bar and ate it. When he returned to the truck, happy voices were coming through the open pool hall door. Two more men had joined the group. One was slapping Mr. Albrecht on the back and he was reaching for his pocketbook and calling for the bartender. It looked as if they were going to be there for a while, so Vic decided to walk around the block.

As he approached the pool hall, the old green Model-T came tearing down the street. Mr. Albrecht's hat brim was pulled low on his forehead and his mustache was blowing in the breeze.

"Hey! Wait a minute," Vic shouted, but Mr. Albrecht sped over the crossing, up the road beyond and disappeared over the top of the hill.

12

Vic stared at the settling dust. He only had himself to blame, he thought despondently. He shouldn't have left the truck.

But maybe Mr. Albrecht really hadn't driven off without him. Maybe he'd gone on another errand and would be coming back. They'd probably know at the pool hall. He decided to go in and inquire.

The pool hall smelled of beer and stale tobacco smoke. It was quiet now and empty of patrons except for an old man dozing in a chair against the wall behind a billiard table. The attendant was washing glasses in a sink at the end of the counter. He looked up when Vic came in. "Sorry," he said, "no one under twenty-one allowed in here."

"Is Mr. Albrecht coming back?"

"I doubt it. He spent all his money, so I guess he went home."

"He was supposed to take me with him."

151

"He probably forgot all about you. He couldn't hit the floor with his hat when he left here."

"Do you know where his place is?"

"Out in the sagebrush down by Moses Lake. Follow the road that crosses the tracks over by the depot until you get to his mailbox. You can't miss the place. The orchard is to the left and there's a big haystack behind the house."

"Thanks. I guess I'd better start walking."

"It's close to thirty miles out there."

"Somebody will probably come along and give me a lift."

"Good luck!"

It wasn't noon yet, and even if he didn't get a ride he should be at the Albrechts by dark—provided his shoes held out. But he couldn't walk thirty miles on an empty stomach.

Vic went into the store next to the pool hall and bought two candy bars. He stopped at the depot and had a drink of water at the fountain in the waiting room, then crossed the tracks and started up the dusty hill. It was short but steep; before he reached the top he was breathing hard and sweating. He broke over the crest, and when he saw what lay ahead, he almost turned around and went back down again.

Left and right and straight ahead, as far as he could see, there was nothing but sagebrush and tumbleweed. The land was low and rolling like swells on an empty sea, with here and there islands of black rock thrust up through the sandy soil. Through heat waves rising from the desert, a range of purple mountains shimmered on the horizon. But in all that vacant land there was not a tree or house. He thought again of turning back and taking his chances with the railroad. Then he thought of the twenty a month and room and board, and kept on going.

Telegraph poles and a power line paralleled the road; as Vic passed each pole he counted it, and when he came to twenty he put a pebble in his pocket. There were supposed to be twenty poles to a mile, so when he had thirty stones he'd know he was near his destination.

Over the crests and down in the hollows, on and on he went. He had long since taken off his mackinaw and was carrying it over his arm. The twine that held the sole on his shoe was wearing well, but now and then a rock got in and he had to stop and shake it out.

He had picked up his seventh pebble and was beginning to feel almost unendurably thirsty when rounding a curve he saw Mr. Albrecht's Model-T sitting out in the sagebrush beside the road. Mr. Albrecht was slumped over the wheel.

At first Vic thought there'd been an accident, but the rancher didn't appear to be hurt, just sound asleep. Vic tried to wake him but he was too far gone for that. There was no use standing around waiting for him to sleep it off. They might be here till dark. He'd better try to get the truck started and back on the road.

Mr. Albrecht was not a large man, but he was so

completely relaxed that getting him out of the driver's seat was like trying to move a 150-pound sack of meal. Vic managed it by grabbing hold of the seat of his overalls and dragging him over to the right-hand side, where he propped him up in the corner.

The truck had stalled in high gear. He put it into neutral, reset the switch and levers, and gave the crank a flip. The engine started and he climbed in over Mr. Albrecht's sprawled legs and slid under the wheel. Soon the truck was rattling down the crooked, bumpy road.

Miles of monotonous landscape went by with little variation except for an occasional cultivated area. The farms all looked alike—house, barn and windmill—and from a distance it was hard to tell whether they were inhabited or deserted. Then Vic noticed that some of them had irrigation ditches, the water glistening in the sunlight, and when he came closer he could see that these fields were green and the orchards well tended. Wherever these fingers of water appeared, the land came alive, though all the surrounding land was sagebrush desert.

At each mailbox Vic slowed down to read the name on it. Long-legged jack rabbits bounded across the road and proud Chinese pheasant cocks in gaudy colors stepped haughtily aside and watched the truck go by. There were some dull-plumaged hens, almost invisible against the gray-green of the sagebrush, and a thick-bodied snake with a vivid pattern on its back slithered across the roadway. Vic, who didn't even like garter snakes, couldn't keep from shuddering when he saw the rattles on its tail.

Farther down the road a cloud of dust appeared, and then a horse and rider came into view, followed by a band of sheep. The bearded sheepherder held up a warning hand and nodded his thank-you as Vic stopped to let him ride by. The flock, guarded by two black-and-white collies, split and flowed around the truck, baaing loudly. A third dog cut back and forth behind the sheep, prodding the laggards from the brush. Vic drove on and Mr. Albrecht never wakened.

A few miles more, and a row of poplars and a windmill tower rose up from the rolling prairie. Then a giant haystack, a water tank, and an orchard pink with blossoms came into view, partly hiding the ugliness of unpainted outbuildings and a house covered with tar paper. The mailbox at the entrance to the side road bore weathered letters reading, "W. Albrecht."

Vic turned in.

Sleek brown hogs rooting in an alfalfa field looked up at the truck's approach and an ugly boar with curving yellow tusks charged, while the little pigs ran off squealing. Vic almost went into a ditch avoiding the boar, and then scattered a flock of varicolored chickens pecking in the dooryard. As he braked to a stop by the back door and shut off the engine, two bulky horses, standing behind a nearby fence, whinnied and stamped their heavy feet.

Goats were everywhere, on the roofs and up the trees, bleating nannies and frisky kids. But as he looked about Vic saw that the cats outnumbered the goats.

A Barred Rock rooster strutted up, cocked his head and looked Vic over, then crowed in a manner that left no doubt as to who was boss around this spread.

Spotting some loose grain that had apparently fallen from the truck, the rooster gave the familiar chirring sound Vic had often heard at home when Struttin' Sam found a choice tidbit for his flock. Hens and chicks came scurrying at the call to gobble up the treat while the rooster stood gallantly aside and watched them. When they'd eaten what they wanted, he pecked up the rest.

Vic recalled a saying of his mother. "If more men would be the gentlemen that roosters are, there would be fewer unhappy women in the world."

A screen door slammed and a stout, blue-eyed woman with untidy hair, wearing a shapeless dress and men's work shoes, stood a moment with hands on hips, glaring toward the truck. As she strode across the farmyard the goats galloped off into the orchard, the chickens cackled and scattered and the rooster flew up onto the water tank. The kittens vanished and the tomcat slunk under a lilac bush. Only the big black police dog, chained to the corner of the house, remained. He stopped barking and flattened into the shadows and lay there trembling.

Vic watched with interest. Animals were sensitive to the moods and emotions of humans. He had noticed it many times at home. When a family fight was brewing the cows were nervous and held back their milk, the chickens frightened easily and the egg production stopped. And it was the same here.

Ignoring Vic, the woman shouted at the figure slumped in the seat beside him. "Ach! You spend my egg money for drink again, I bet!"

She shook Mr. Albrecht hard until he opened his eyes. He put up his arms defensively. "I'm sorry, Mama! I won't do it again!"

"Always you are sorry! Always you do it again!"

Mr. Albrecht stumbled out of the car and staggered off to the water tower, turned on a faucet and put his head under it.

Mrs. Albrecht turned and glared at Vic. "Where did you come from?"

"Ephrata. Your husband gave me a job."

"If you stay here you got to work."

"That's what I came for, Ma'am."

The flush of anger left her face. "You come," she said. "I'll show you where to sleep."

Vic picked up his coat and got out of the truck.

"I'd like to get a drink of water first," he said.

She waited while he went to the faucet beneath the tank. The water had a brackish odor, but he drank what seemed like a gallon. Then he followed the woman to a small shed between two poplars.

The one room contained a rusty sheet-iron heating stove, a sagging cot with patchwork quilts, and an apple box with some old magazines piled on it. A small light bulb dangled overhead. The room looked and smelled as though it had once been a chicken coop. There were feathers on the floor, so chickens must still use it on occasion. There was one grimy window and the rafters were festooned with dusty cobwebs.

Vic dropped his coat on the cot and looked at the floor. "Do you have a broom I can use?"

"After supper you can sweep it. You come. I'll show you some work to do."

Vic balked. "I'm sorry, lady, but I've got to have something to eat first."

"Didn't Papa buy you some lunch?"

"No, Ma'am."

She glowered toward the water tank and muttered something under her breath. "You come. I get you something." She went toward the screen door to the kitchen and opened it.

There was a cookstove, cupboard, table, several rickety chairs and a couch. A battery radio with horn-type loud-speaker was on the table and an enlarged and tinted snapshot of three children stood on the cluttered windowsill. The linoleum on the floor was worn and faded, spotted here and there with tracked-in dirt. Fuzzy balls of lint and litter had collected in the corners and underneath the stove and table.

"You can sit down," she said, and took a pitcher of milk and a glass from the cupboard. She cut some slices from a loaf of bread and put them on a plate before him. The milk had an odd taste he wasn't used to. It must be goat's milk. Too hungry to be choosy, he gulped it down and wolfed the bread.

Mrs. Albrecht sat down across the table. "What is your name?"

"Vic Martin, Ma'am."

"Do you have a mudder?"

His mouth too full to speak, he nodded.

"Does she know where you are?"

He shook his head and poured more milk, trying not to see the goat hair in it. Ugh! No wonder the rancher had to come to jail to get his help. The local people probably knew how it was out here.

Mrs. Albrecht interrupted his thoughts. "Why did you leave your home, Wiktor?"

"To find a job."

"Did your mudder cry when you went away?"

"I don't know." He hadn't thought of that.

She leaned across the table and shook a finger at him. "You probably broke your mudder's heart." She touched the photo on the windowsill, turned it so the meager light would strike it better. It was of two boys and a girl, all very young.

"Are those your children, Ma'am?"

She nodded. "They growed up and went away." She dropped her hands into her lap and stared at the picture as though not seeing it at all, but rather something very far away. "Children always break their mudder's heart."

Vic ate the rest of the bread in silence and drank

all but the last inch of milk in the bottom of the pitcher.

When he had finished, Mrs. Albrecht looked at the empty glass and bread plate. "You had enough?"

"Yes, Ma'am."

They got up from the table and left the house. As they passed the water tank Mr. Albrecht raised his head. "I got your flour and sugar for you, Mama."

She walked on, pretending not to hear.

Louder, he said, "I got the spray, too."

"Then you had better start to spray!" she snapped.

She stopped by a dry irrigation ditch at the edge of the orchard. The ground beneath the trees ahead was a tangle of pruned-off limbs. "You pick up all the branches in one row and pile them in the next row," she said to Vic. "Do you understand?"

"Yes, Ma'am."

"You put the big sticks in a different pile for stove-wood, and you do a real good job. We got no time for loafers here."

"Yes, Ma'am." Vic spoke politely but he had already decided he would be on his way again in the morning. Meanwhile, though, he'd get started picking up some of that brush.

13

Vic had been working less than two hours but it seemed like four. He hadn't finished half a row yet and there must be a good thirty more to go. He straightened his aching back and twisted his head and shoulders to try to take the stiffness from his muscles. Picking up brush was as bad as digging clams. It wasn't just his back that ached but the tendons in his legs as well.

The sun was getting so low it *must* be near quitting time.

He gathered another armload of branches and threw them on the pile. Turning, he saw Mr. Albrecht slouching toward him down the row. It occurred to Vic that his stooped shoulders had probably come from years of bending in this orchard. The rancher stopped and looked around. "Another week you'll be done."

You've got a surprise coming tomorrow, Mister, Vic thought.

"Come. The old woman's got supper almost ready."

They started for the house. When they'd walked a few yards, Mr. Albrecht cocked a bloodshot eye at Vic. "How did you get here, anyway?"

Vic told him.

"I guess that new beer was stronger than I thought." He took a drink at the faucet and went on to the house.

Vic stayed at the water tank to wash. He combed his hair, then went to the door and rapped. "Come in," Mrs. Albrecht called. "You don't have to knock."

A glance at the stove and the smell of the kitchen told him they were having boiled potatoes, fried salt pork, and coffee. There were sliced raw onions and bread on the table. The floor looked as though it had been swept, and Mrs. Albrecht was wearing a clean dress. Her hair was combed and done up in a bun.

"You sit right down," she said. "Supper is almost ready." Her husband was already seated, fiddling with the dials of the radio.

Vic took a chair. Through the unwashed window he could see a spectacular sunset spreading over the Cascades in the west, low now, and far away.

There was a burst of static from the loud-speaker horn, and a news commentator for a Seattle station came on. "Here is the news as of six o'clock P.M., Friday, April 28th, 1933. Japanese armies are pushing back the Chinese north of Peiping and the capture of the ancient capital is imminent. One hundred earthquakes have been registered in Alaska. New enrollees of the Civilian Conservation Corps are crowding Army garrisons across the country. In the American League the Yankees beat the Athletics, five to two; in the National League, the Cubs three, Pirates two. It looks as if the wet spell has broken. The Weather Bureau predicts tomorrow fair and sunny."

It was the first news Vic had heard since he'd left home, but apparently he hadn't missed much.

The rancher turned off the radio and Mrs. Albrecht filled the plates at the stove and set them on the table.

Vic got the biggest potatoes and the largest chunk of meat. The potatoes had been cooked with the jackets on. There was nothing wrong with that, but the bad spots hadn't been cut out first. The salt pork was almost solid fat and the rancid smell of the meat reached him before the first forkful was halfway to his mouth. He hesitated, but the Albrechts apparently weren't concerned. They were devouring pork rind and all. Vic held his breath, popped the bite into his mouth, gulped and reached for a slice of raw onion. The onion was hot and strong and killed the taste of the meat. He skinned a potato and cut into it. Only half cooked, it had a "bone" in the center. Mrs. Albrecht sure could use some cooking lessons. Why, he'd eaten a lot better than this from Curly's boilin'-up can! He tried not to think of his mother's cooking.

Mr. Albrecht ate fast, as though to get it over with, and then lighted his pipe and got up. "I go work on my sprayer now." He reached for his hat. "Come out to the shed when you finish eating. I'll give you a lantern and you can pick up brush till bedtime."

"I kind of thought I was all through for the day."

"I can't drive my sprayer down the rows till the brush gets picked up, and I got to spray next week or the codling moth might get into the fruit." He left the house.

When Vic's plate was empty, he declined the second helping Mrs. Albrecht offered him, although he was still hungry. He excused himself and went outside. A light was burning in one of the outbuildings and there was a sound of hammering when Vic got there. Mr. Albrecht was taking apart an old gasoline-powered pump mounted on the rear of a big, horse-drawn tank wagon.

"Having trouble?"

The rancher whacked the cylinder of the rusty engine angrily with his ball-peen hammer. "Everything is all wore out! If I don't get good prices for my fruit this year, I'm going to let the bank have the place!" He threw the hammer down and picked up a wrench.

"Where's that lantern, Mr. Albrecht?"

"Over there on a nail. You got matches?"

"No."

The rancher handed over a penny box of matches. Vic lighted the wick of the lantern, lowered the chimney and put the matchbox in his pocket. He went to the place where he'd been working before supper and hung the lantern on a limb. It cast just enough light for him to pick up brush by. But Vic was in no hurry to begin. He sat down with his back to a tree.

Where would he be this time tomorrow? He sat thinking and listening to the night sounds.

"Wiktor!"

Vic opened his eyes and looked up at a bobbing lantern that was coming toward him. He must have been dozing.

"Where are you, Wiktor?" It was Mrs. Albrecht. Before he could get up and grab some brush she was there. "Why aren't you working?"

"Well, I . . ." He pointed downward. The twine that kept the sole from flapping was worn almost through. "I was just fixing my shoe." He began working at the knot.

She held her lantern close. "Is that the only shoes you have?"

"Yes, Ma'am." He unwound the twine, broke the worn places and tied them together again.

She lowered her voice. "I got some money put away that Papa doesn't know about. In the morning you pick some shoes out of the catalog and we'll send an order to Sears Roebuck."

"That would sure be nice." He got to his feet.

"But you'll have to pay me back out of what you earn."

"Yes, Ma'am. That's fair enough with me."

She hung her lantern from a tree. "I come out to help you a little bit." She began to pick up brush.

Vic went to work. "At home we used to pick up right after pruning time."

"Papa always puts things off till it's almost too late." She threw an armload on the pile. "If the orchard inspectors find the codling moth in our trees, they'll have them cut down and burned."

"Is it that serious?"

"The codling moth is a terrible thing, Wiktor, terrible."

So if he left before the brush was picked up, the trees couldn't be sprayed in time to prevent the codling moth and the orchard might have to be destroyed. So what! It wasn't his fault that Mr. Albrecht hadn't cleaned out his rows when he should have. Let the codling moth have the place.

But, on the other hand, how long was it since he'd had brand new shoes of his own and not someone else's misfitting, worn-out hand-me-downs? Maybe he'd better wait until the shoes got here. Tomorrow would be Saturday, and even if the order went out right away he probably wouldn't get the shoes before next Saturday. But it would be worth sticking it out till then and in the meantime he'd have the brush picked up. He threw an armload on the pile and bent for another.

When they reached the end of the row, Mrs. Albrecht said, "This is enough for today."

They took their lanterns back to the shed, blew them out, and hung them up. The engine from the sprayer was all in pieces on the floor. Mr. Albrecht had one part in a vise and was working at it with a file and muttering, "Everything is all wore out!"

Outside, Mrs. Albrecht said, "We could buy everything new with what he has spent for drink."

Vic went with her to the back door. "Could I borrow your catalog? Maybe I could pick out those shoes tonight."

She brought the book. "Do you want a glass of milk before you go to bed?"

"No, thanks." He put the catalog under his arm and went off to his chicken coop.

The door was open. Inside, the aroma of chickens was gone and it smelled like his mother's kitchen after she'd scrubbed the floor with lye water. He found the dangling light bulb in the darkness overhead and snapped it on. The floor had been scrubbed and was still damp in places. The window had been washed, too, and the cobwebs had been swept from the rafters. His coat was hung on a nail, the bed had been remade and the featherbed fluffed up. He closed the door, undressed, and climbed in between the blankets. He sank down into the feathers. Boy, what comfort!

He opened the catalog to Men's Work Shoes. The best-looking pair was the most expensive: $3.69, postpaid. Those were the ones he wanted, but what a price to pay for shoes. "Black blucher with Compo sole; double-tanned overweight barnyard-proof uppers; heavy grain leather insoles." They were probably worth it.

A more reasonable pair was pictured below. "Knockout blow to wear and tear; full double leather soles; extra outside sole of tough Compo." They were $2.39, postpaid. Maybe he'd better order the cheaper ones and spend the difference on socks. The pair he had were full of holes. He looked at socks. He could get three pairs for eighty-nine cents.

He turned to Guns. There was a Long Tom shotgun he'd like to have, and a 30-30 Winchester rifle. It would be great to be rich . . .

The catalog slipped from his fingers and he heard it hit the floor. He should get up and turn the light off but he didn't want to lose the wonderful sensation of drifting off to sleep.

He was awakened by the sound of someone chopping wood. Sunlight was coming through the window and he smelled the pungent smoke from a newly started fire. The rooster crowed, the hens clucked, and chicks peeped. He knew it was probably time he got up, too. But the bed was warm and the room was chilly, so he decided to stay put until someone called him. He didn't have long to wait. The kitchen door slammed and heavy footsteps crunched across the farmyard. There was a rap on the door. "Are you awake yet, Wiktor?"

"I was just about to get up, Mrs. Albrecht."

She came in, carrying some folded clothing. "You wear some of Papa's things today and I'll wash yours."

She put the clothes on the foot of the bed and picked up his shirt and overalls and socks. "You bring me your underwear when you come to breakfast." She left the shed.

Vic was ashamed to have anyone see the BVD's he was wearing. Like his socks, they were so full of holes they looked like lacework. He sat up and reached for the old-fashioned long-johns Mrs. Albrecht had left. He put them on.

The sleeves of the one-piece suit ended halfway between his wrist and elbow. The legs hit him just below the knees. He had to stoop his shoulders to get them buttoned. The shirt sleeves were no better a fit than those of the long-johns, and he had to let the straps of the bib overalls all the way out to get them hooked. When he was dressed, there were a good six inches of bare legs showing between sock tops and the hems of the overall legs.

After washing at the water tank Vic went to the kitchen. He was hungry and looking forward to the coffee and fried eggs he could smell. It was hard to ruin good, fresh eggs, Vic thought, but one look at the plate Mrs. Albrecht set before him and he saw that she had managed it. They'd been cooked too long and too early, and were hard and cold. He tried the coffee. It was undercooked, weak and full of floating grounds.

At Mrs. Albrecht's second call, her husband came in, wolfed his eggs, gulped his coffee, and went back to his pounding in the shed. When he had gone she put the skillet on again. "I get something for me now."

Vic jumped up. "Why don't you let me fix your breakfast?"

"Oh, boys don't know how to cook."

"Well, I do. I've been helping my mother in the kitchen since I was little." He steered her to a chair and she sat down.

He took a lid off the stove, threw in some sticks of chopped-up apple limbs and opened the drafts. When the fire was going well he passed a hand over the stove and felt for a hot spot. He put the coffee pot there—maybe he could still do something with it. The pot began to boil and after a minute or two he took it off and put in some cold water. He set it aside for the grounds to settle. The grease in the skillet started smoking and he reached for the bucket of eggs on the table. "How many do you want?"

"T'ree will be good. And you have more yourself."

Vic broke six eggs into a bowl, dumped them into the sizzling skillet. "How do you like them, sunny side up or over easy?"

"Oh, just any way."

He put on a sprinkling of salt and a dusting of pepper, and when the whites had lost their transparency he separated the eggs with the turner. He put three on a plate and set it in front of Mrs. Albrecht, the other three on his own. He filled the cups. The coffee was darker now and the grounds were absent. He sat down and tied into his second batch of eggs.

She took a bite. "This is real good, Wiktor. What did you do?"

"There's nothing to it, Ma'am. Just don't cook them too long, and serve them hot." When he'd cleaned his plate he said, "Shall I go get the catalog now so we can make out the order for those shoes?"

"Shoes? What shoes?"

Could she have forgotten already, or was she going to back out on the deal? "Remember last night you said we'd send to Sears Roebuck and get me some shoes?" He held up a foot. "These are about shot."

She looked at the torn shoe and frowned.

"Shall I get the catalog?"

"Yes, you get the catalog. It just slipped my mind."

When he got back he showed her the shoes he wanted. "But they're expensive. Maybe I'd better get these cheaper ones down here."

"No, you get the good ones. They will last longer."

"And I need some socks."

"You get them, too."

He tore an order blank from the catalog. "Do you have a pen?"

She pawed through the things on the windowsill and found an indelible pencil.

"What is the address here, Ma'am?"

"Star Route, Ephrata, Washington."

One pair shoes, $3.69; three pairs socks, 89 cents.

He added it and wrote the total at the bottom. "There it is, Mrs. Albrecht, $4.58." He handed her the order.

"I will take it to the box when I see the mailman coming."

Vic started to get up. "I guess I'd better go out in the orchard and start earning it."

She put a hand on his arm. "You should write a letter to your poor mudder and tell her where you are."

"I don't have a paper or a stamp or anything."

She found a scratch pad on the windowsill. "Here is paper and I will get you an envelope. You tell your mudder we are good, hard-working Christian people and for her not to worry about you."

From the shed there came a burst of most un-Christian sounds. Mr. Albrecht must have hit his finger. Vic wrote the letter.

Ephrata, Wash.

Dear Mom,

I'll bet you never heard of this place, did you? Neither had I until I got stranded here by a freight train a couple of nights ago. Yesterday morning a rancher, Mr. Albrecht, gave me a job. I think the Albrechts are Germans. They have a big orchard and lots of stock. They're going to pay me twenty dollars a month. The grub isn't very good, though. Mrs. A. could sure take some lessons from *you*.

She is sending to Sears today to get me some new shoes and socks. By the way, would you go through

the rag bag and see if you can find a shirt and overalls and some underwear that might fit me? A guy
stole all my things in Seattle. I could use a bar of soap
and a towel, too, if you could spare some.

Your loving son, Vic
P.S.: They weren't taking any enlistments in the Navy.
I'd like to get in one of those CCC camps so I might
not stay here very long. Love.

He addressed the envelope, put the letter in, and
sealed it. "Will you mail this when you send the
order, Mrs. Albrecht?"

"Your mudder will be happy to hear from you,
Wiktor. My children hardly ever write to me."

He went out to the shed. Mr. Albrecht was bolting
the engine together.

"Do you want me to keep on picking up brush?"
Vic asked.

"Yah, but first you hitch up the horses to that
stoneboat over by the stable and then load that stuff
you piled up yesterday. Take it out in the sagebrush
and dump it."

The stoneboat was a low, wide sled with wooden
runners. It had racks on either side for carrying bulky
loads. Vic shook out the reins and clucked to the
team. "Giddap!" The horses leaned into their collars
and with shod hoofs clopping they dragged the
stoneboat across the farmyard and into the orchard.

When the racks would hold no more Vic drove to

the end of the row and out into the sagebrush. Circles of ashes and charred branch ends showed where there had been fires in other years. He pulled up beside one of the spots and unloaded.

He had finished and was about to drive off when he heard the crow of a Chinese pheasant cock. He wrapped the reins around the end of the rack and got off the stoneboat. Picking up three fair-sized stones, he crouched down and began creeping through the sage. He stopped, listened. The sound was nearer, but to his left. He circled around so the sun would be behind him, heard the crow again, moved toward it.

Vic saw the pheasant just as it lifted from the ground and let fly with a stone. He hit the bird with the first try, and it fell to the ground. He picked it up and hung it high in a tree where it couldn't be seen. He wished pheasant cocks weren't so pretty. Killing one was almost as bad as killing a deer. But nature had made them tasty and he was hungry.

Vic went back to picking up brush. Now that he had his dinner, how was he going to cook it? Roasting over the coals called for constant watching and turning, so that was out. He could pack the bird in mud and bury it in hot ashes, but that took too long. Boiling was the answer. But in what? He'd have to look around and see what he could find when he went in at noon. He'd need a fire, too, but that was simple. He still had the matches he'd been given to light the lantern last night.

The work went well, despite his sore back, and by midmorning Vic was starting on the third row when he saw Mrs. Albrecht coming through the trees. Kaiser, the dog, was bounding ahead of her and a procession of cats, goats, chickens, and geese came along behind. He stopped working and stretched his back while he waited for her. She had some letters in one hand and a pint fruit jar full of milk in the other. She handed him the jar.

"I thought you might like something about now, Wiktor."

He did, but not goat milk. "Well, gee, thanks." As soon as she was gone he'd dump it out. "I think I'll finish this row first." He started to set the jar in the crotch of a tree.

"You drink it right now so I can have the jar."

"I'll bring the jar when I come in at noon."

"No, maybe you'll forget. I'll wait while you drink it."

He knew he had to drink it if it killed him, so he took off the lid, shut his eyes, and began to gulp. The milk was so fresh it was still warm. He emptied the jar in one draught and handed it back. "That was good." And it *was* good!

She looked through the orchard and out across the sagebrush toward a plume of dust rising in the distance. "That must be the letter carrier coming. I better go to the mailbox now." She looked around. "Where are you, Kaiser?" The dog was down at the far end of the row sniffing underneath a tree. He licked at the ground, then looked up into the branches. "What's the matter with that dog?" she said. "He acts like there is a bird up in that tree."

Vic grinned and went back to work.

14

The sun was high when Mr. Albrecht came to the orchard. He looked around but made no comment about the four rows Vic had finished. "The old woman has dinner ready. Turn the team loose and come in."

Vic unhooked the horses, took the bits from their mouths and coiled the reins around the hames. They began to graze amid the trees. "Won't they stray off?"

"They won't go away. This is the only green grass for miles."

"Do you want me to start burning that brush I've got piled up out there?" Vic asked as they walked to the house.

"If the wind is blowing away from my orchard, you burn it, yah."

The kitchen had the delicious smell of fresh bread, and a loaf, hot out of the oven, was on the table. To Vic's surprise it tasted as good as it smelled. Mrs. Albrecht could really bake bread and he told her so as he reached for another slice.

"Have some of that blut sausage with it."

He cut a small piece off the long, black rope. It was good, hard and spicy. There was some homemade cheese on the table, too, sharp and tangy. But he liked the sausage best and kept going back for more. "What did you call this?"

"Blut sausage."

"What's it made of?"

"Blut—the blut from the pig."

"Blut? You mean blood?"

"Yah, we save the blut and make sausage with it. You want some more?"

"No thanks. I'm full now."

Mr. Albrecht got up from the table. "I go take my nap." He went into the other room and they heard him lie down on a squeaky bed.

"Do you want to take a nap, too, Wiktor?" Mrs. Albrecht asked.

"I think I'll go out and start burning that brush."

"You don't have to go back to work till one o'clock."

"Oh, that's all right. I like to work with fires."

"You make sure the wind isn't blowing toward the orchard."

He nodded. "Say, do you have a pail or something I could take some drinking water out in?"

"There is buckets in the shed. Help yourself."

"Could I have a little handful of salt, too?"

"What do you want salt for?"

"Well, uh . . . I, well, I'm not used to this warm weather. I've heard you should eat salt when you're sweating a lot."

She pointed to the salt sack in the cupboard. "Help yourself." He took a big handful and left.

There were buckets in the shed, all right, and they were dirty. He scoured one at the faucet, filled it half full of water, and went out to the brush piles. He got several big fires going; then he built a small one off by itself and circled it with stones. He set the bucket of water on the stones to heat, and went to the apple tree and got his pheasant. He plucked it and burned the feathers, took out the insides, cut it apart and dropped the pieces in the water. He added some salt and sat down to watch it.

When the pounding began in the shed again, Vic caught the horses and went back to his branch gathering. Each time he brought a load to burn he added a few sticks to his cooking fire. In the late afternoon the bird was cooked, and with each trip to the fires he ate a piece. By quitting time the pail was empty except for the broth and he drank that. He unhooked the team and drove to the watering trough, not caring what was on the table for supper.

Mr. Albrecht came out of the shed. "How many rows today?"

"Eight." In two more days the job would be done, and when the shoes and socks came he could leave with a clear conscience.

Mrs. Albrecht had to shake Vic hard to rouse him in the morning. "Are you going to sleep all day, Wiktor?"

"What time is it?"

"Eight o'clock."

"Gosh, you should have called me earlier."

"It is Sunday. You don't have to work today." She handed him his clean clothes. "We are having pancakes for breakfast."

When she had gone, he got up and took off Mr. Albrecht's underwear. After his wearing them for twenty-four hours they'd never be the same again. He put his washed and mended BVD's on. Mrs. Albrecht had even darned his socks, sewed a couple of missing buttons on his shirt, and patched the hole that George Brown had slit in his overall pocket.

They had finished eating when he got to the house. Mr. Albrecht was smoking his pipe and looking at the Sunday paper that had come in the mail the day before. His wife had her glasses on and was reading from a Bible printed in German. There were plenty of pancakes left. They were big and heavy, and tasted as if they might have been fried the night before and warmed over in the oven. But sprinkled with sugar and followed by coffee they weren't too bad. When the pancakes were all gone, Vic read the Sunday funnies.

Mr. Albrecht looked up from the magazine section he was reading. "Wiktor, what is a light-year?"

"A light-year?"

The rancher tapped the paper with his pipestem. "It says here that some of the stars are a hundred light-years away. I don't know what is a light-year."

Pleased that he should be asked the question and glad that he knew the answer, Vic said, "I learned in physics that a light-year is the distance light travels in one year—at the rate of 186,000 miles a second. You multiply that by the number of seconds in a year." He reached for the pencil and tablet on the window-sill. "Sixty seconds in a minute, sixty minutes in an hour, 24 hours in a day, 365 days in a year . . ."

"That would be about six trillion miles," Mr. Albrecht said.

Vic finished his computations. "Why that's exactly right. Did you figure that out in your head?"

"Why, sure."

"Boy, I wish I could do that."

Mrs. Albrecht beamed. "Papa is awful good with figures."

"I never did like arithmetic very well."

"You should learn all about numbers that you can," Mr. Albrecht said. "It comes in handy."

When Vic was finished with the funnies, he stood up and stretched.

"What are you going to do today?" Mrs. Albrecht asked.

"Oh, I don't know."

"Do you like to fish?"

"I sure do."

"There are lots of fish in Moses Lake. It's about a mile down that old road behind the stable."

"Do you have any fishing tackle?"

"My boy's pole is out in the shed someplace."

He hesitated. "I don't know if my shoes will stand the walk."

Mr. Albrecht put down his paper. "There is an old

pair of shoes out in my feed room that an apple-knocker left here one time. Go put them on." Vic went out the door and the rancher called after him, "You feed and water my horses while you are there, too."

The apple-knocker's shoes were buried in a dusty pile of old horse collars and harness straps in a corner of the feed room. When he picked them up, a mouse ran out of one. The shoes were green with mold, hard as iron, and the toes had curled up until they looked like a sultan's sandals. They might fit but he couldn't even try to put them on until they'd been softened a bit. He shook out the trash the mice had stored in them and put rocks inside. Then he put them in the watering trough to soak until tomorrow morning, and tied new sack twine around his old shoes. They'd get him to the lake and back.

After he'd cared for the horses he found the fishing pole, dug a can of worms in the orchard, and headed along the pair of crooked ruts behind the stable. They led him down a coulee through the arid, brush-grown desertland to a road that angled up a hillside. At the top was an old deserted farmhouse with a neglected orchard and a rusty windmill. The lake was below. Narrow and meandering, it was more like a blue and silent river, bordered by a narrow strip of green.

Vic went down the hill to a willow clump at the water's edge and sat down on a rock in the shade. He baited his hook, threw it into an opening in the lily pads, and immediately caught a turtle—something you didn't catch at home. Maybe he'd keep it for a pet. He removed the hook as gently as he could, but the turtle bit his finger. Such gratitude! He threw it back into the water.

Next he caught a catfish, then a bass, several carp, and finally a trout. More turtles, more carp, more catfish, bass, and another trout. The hook snagged on the bottom, and when he took his shoes and socks off and waded out to free it, he found the water so warm he undressed and had a swim.

Afterward he sat in the sun to dry.

When he had dressed again he gathered some dead willows, built a fire, and roasted and ate his trout. He stretched out and had a nap, then fished again. But he caught fish so fast it took all the fun out of it, and by midafternoon he'd lost interest in fishing. He cleaned his fish, strung them on a willow, and went back to the ranch.

Mrs. Albrecht was very pleased. "You are a good fisherman, Wiktor." She fed the carp to the cats, scaled the trout and bass and skinned the catfish. "We will have them for supper."

Vic prowled around and found some flexible wire. He made some snares and went out and set them in rabbit runs in the sagebrush. He came back through the orchard and found a branch with a good crotch. Using strips cut from an old inner tube he'd found in the shed, he made a slingshot.

When he got up on Monday morning Vic went to the watering trough and got the apple-knocker's shoes. They were a little on the snug side but he could wear them, so he threw his old ones away.

Wednesday morning he reached the last two rows of the orchard and found that they were cherry trees, not apple. The blossoms had all fallen and the fruit was already well developed. Things certainly matured earlier east of the mountains than they did over on the coast. When he'd left home the vegetables were just pushing through the ground.

In the big truck garden over beyond the Albrecht house, the green onions and new carrots were almost ready, the potato plants were knee-high, and the corn was up. There was a lot to be said for this part of the country. It was too bad the hills were so far away and there were no woods or beaches. But you couldn't have everything, and he'd snared two fat rabbits during the night.

He had dropped down to rest for a few minutes when he saw Mrs. Albrecht coming toward him, escorted by a procession of goats, cats, chickens, a pig or two, and the dog. She always went to the mailbox in midmorning, and today she had a letter for him. "I think it's from your mudder." Vic wrapped the reins around the rack and opened the envelope.

Gardiner, Wash.

Dear Son:

We were awfully sorry to find you gone the other morning. We didn't realize how much those boards meant to you.

I know you can take care of yourself, but I'm glad I didn't know you were riding freight trains or I would have worried.

It's nice that you have a job. There's more work opening up here, too. Mr. Gardiner is going to put in another twenty acres of berries so there will be lots of weekend work, now.

Fred has been trying to help with the milking but he can't seem to get the knack of it.

We all miss you. Especially Jack. He sits by the gate looking up the road all the time.

Your loving Mother

Vic folded the letter slowly and put it into his pocket. *We all miss you.* Those four words eased the sore spot that had been burning inside of him since the morning he left home. He bent and scooped up an armload of brush.

By noon the last of the branches was picked up, and after lunch they started spraying. The tank wagon was filled with water, and arsenate of lead and sulphur was dumped in. The team was hitched and Vic and Mr. Albrecht drove to the orchard. They smeared their hands and faces with lard and started the pump. Mr. Albrecht sprayed the first tree, watched Vic do the second, then went back to the shed to repair a broken plow. Fighting the heavy nozzle that jetted the bad-smelling solution was hard, unpleasant work. Vic was glad when it was six o'clock.

When he started again the next morning Vic worked fast, anxious to get the miserable job over and done with. He didn't stop to do anything but refill the tank. Two more days passed in this way. On Friday morning Mrs. Albrecht came back from the mailbox. She brought two packages. One was professionally packed and had a typed label. It was from Sears.

The other was wrapped in insufficient paper and tied with kinky string raveled from a flour sack. Even without looking at the penciled handwriting he knew where it was from. All his mother's parcels had that flimsy, sagging look, even before she mailed them. He opened it first. Inside were a pair of heavy duty overalls, a blue work shirt, two union suits, three pairs of socks, all brand new! How in the world had she managed this? A note tucked into the shirt pocket explained it: "I was in Mr. Frank's store yesterday. He said he'd given you a ride to Seattle. Wanted to know if I'd heard from you. Told him you had a job but your clothes were stolen. He said to send you these. Pay for them when you're able. The soap and doughnuts are from Marie."

In among the clothes there was a grease-stained paper sack. It contained a bar of soap and dried-up crumblings of what had been the doughnuts. He tried some of them. But they tasted soapy, and he fed them to the pigs.

He opened the mail-order parcel. The shoes were everything the catalog had said and then some. He looked them over admiringly, rubbing a hand across the shiny black toes and savoring the smell of the new leather. He sat down and tried them on. The fit was perfect. But they were too nice to wear to work. He'd save them to wear on special occasions. He'd save the new clothes, too. He did put on a new pair of socks. After all, he had six pairs.

He wrote to his mother that night to thank her for the parcel.

He added a postscript: "Please thank Mr. Frank for me and tell Marie those doughnuts sure were good."

It took a full week to complete the spraying, and another for Vic to plow ditches between the orchard rows for irrigation. The windmill and the shallow well beneath it were used only to keep the tank filled for house and farmyard needs. Irrigation water was pumped by electricity from a deep well behind the shed. Mr. Albrecht complained as he threw the switch that set the pump to humming and water gushed into the main ditch. "There goes more money to the electric company. Always I work for somebody else. If it isn't for the electric company it's for the spray company or the fertilizer people or the apple-knockers and the hired hands. I get nothing."

Unnoticed, his wife had come up to watch the turning-on of the water. "And don't forget the bootleggers, Papa."

The rancher turned and stamped away, mustache bristling.

The hard young fruit had to be thinned, and for days on end it was up and down a ladder from dawn till dusk. When that was done, an alfalfa field had to be mowed, the hay shocked and hauled and stacked, the field disked and irrigated. Ten hours a day, six days a week, Vic finished one job and started another, but the work was never done.

Yet in spite of the long hours and the food that was poorer than anything he'd ever had at home, Vic was more contented than he'd been for a long time. He had a job and he was left alone to do it. If things were not done quite right there were no sharp criticisms, no sarcastic nicknames. And his responsibilities made him feel like a man—something he never felt at home. Often he found himself whistling or singing while he worked.

He kept his snares set; on Sundays he went fishing at the lake and explored the countryside with his slingshot. On one such expedition he met a band of horses at a bend in a coulee. They were unbranded, had long tails and shaggy manes, and were led by a roan stallion.

He was a magnificent animal, a king of the range and he knew it. His glossy coat was marred by battle scars. The shaggy forelock, matted mane and flowing tail added to the impression of his wildness. He was a creature to be admired and feared. Trembling, but awed by the big horse and wanting to be closer to him, Vic put a hand out and took a step toward the wild creature. It switched its tail nervously and made throaty sounds of warning that carried across the hundred yards between them.

Vic took another step, the horse retreated one, looked over its shoulder toward the band galloping off up the dusty coulee. He looked back at Vic, prancing in little circles. "Come on, old fellow," Vic encouraged, "let's be friends." He began walking slowly toward the horse, hand still outstretched. For a moment the stallion stood his ground, breathing deeply, flanks atremble. Then, abruptly curling back his lips, he bared his yellow teeth, shrieked and charged.

Forgetting about rattlesnakes, Vic plunged into the sagebrush and ran behind a head-high rock. The horse stopped beyond it, so close he could smell its sweaty body. It stamped the ground defiantly, gave one last warning snort, then whirled and galloped off after his band of mares and colts. It was easy to believe what he had heard—that the stallion would have given his life in their defense.

When Vic mentioned the horses that evening, Mr. Albrecht said since they were wild, they belonged to anyone who caught them.

The weather remained clear and dry, each day seeming warmer than the one before. On nights when there was no wind, and the shack was stuffy and Vic couldn't sleep, he would take a quilt, stretch out on the ground and watch the stars.

Those were nights for thought. Where would he be now had he built his boat and sailed away, or gotten into the Navy, or the CCC? What if he'd kept traveling with Billie and Curly?

Sometimes he would have again the old dream of how life would have been if his own father had not got discouraged and left them. But there was no use thinking about what might have been. It was things as they were now that he had to deal with and nothing would ever change. Not while this depression lasted, anyway.

But now that he was away from home he could see some things from a different angle. His constant fights with his stepfather, for instance. There'd been times when he'd deliberately started something just to get even with the old man. One thing that always got him when he wasn't working, Vic had discovered, was his whistling as loud as he could, "Everybody Works But Father." And when the old man laced into him, he'd just say, innocently, "What's the matter, Dad? I was only whistling."

"Why do you *do* it, Vic?" his mother used to ask in desperation. "Why do you bait him like that? Don't you know you just make it harder for me?"

He knew, yet he hadn't been able to help himself, and so he wouldn't even admit it. But now, from a safe distance, he had to concede that his mother had been right. At the same time he knew that if he were home again, it would probably be the same as before.

The Albrechts were never idle. No matter how early Vic awakened they were up and busy, and when he went to bed they were still doing chores. Mrs. Albrecht milked the goats, fed the chickens, cared for the garden, chopped the stovewood, washed the clothes. There were even times when she'd bring a shovel and help Vic clean irrigation ditches.

As they worked she talked unceasingly of her troubles—and they were many. "Always be kind to your mudder and your wife, Wiktor," she would say. "Don't you think I'm right?" And Victor would nod or shake his head while the lonely woman told and retold her tales of unhappiness. Then she'd say, "Oh, I talk too much," shoulder her shovel and stride away.

Most of Mr. Albrecht's time was spent in the tool shed, working with wires, hammering and muttering—repairing things, Vic supposed. He mentioned it to Mrs. Albrecht one day and she said, "He is working on his invention."

"What is he inventing?"

"A machine so that when he turns on a light switch the electricity won't show on the meter."

At breakfast on a Saturday morning in the middle of the month, Mr. Albrecht said, "How many eggs do you have, Mama?"

"Just a little over two cases."

Mr. Albrecht pushed his chair back. "I think I will have a good wash and go to town and sell them."

She pushed her chair back, too. "I think I will go with you. Wiktor can look after the place."

When Vic went out, Mr. Albrecht was shaving with a straight razor before a mirror hung from one of the water tank supports. "You go start my truck and bring it over here," he said.

Vic cranked up the engine, drove to the water tank and filled the radiator. He put the cases of eggs on back and tied the tarp over them. Mrs. Albrecht hurried out and climbed into the cab. She was wearing clothes too tight for her and at least fifteen years out of style.

Her husband glanced around from his shaving. "I'm not ready yet."

"I know, but I don't trust you. You drove off without me once."

With soap still in his ears, Mr. Albrecht jammed his hat on, climbed over the spare tire and slid under the wheel. The Model-T lurched forward, scattering squawking chickens as it roared out of the yard. Hanging onto her hat with one hand, Mrs. Albrecht waved to Vic with the other. "I'll bring you something from town!"

After the letter carrier had passed, Vic stopped work and went to the mailbox. Besides the Sunday paper, there was a letter for him. It was from Marie.

Dear Vic:

I'm planning to have a little family get-together on the first Saturday of August, between Mom's and Freddy's birthdays. Uncle Jim and Aunt Rose are coming over and I thought it would be a nice surprise for Mom if you could be there, too. Mom's been kind of under the weather lately. I guess she's just a little more tired than usual on account of the extra work. She's been awfully lonesome for you, and so have the kids. If you can make it, don't mention it because I'd like to have it as a surprise. Uncle Jim says he'll buy the watermelon and ice cream. Our chickens are doing well this year, so there'll be all the thighs and drumsticks you can eat.

Love, Marie

There was a postscript: "I'm making you some undershorts. I hope you don't mind pink because that's all the material I have."

When the truck rattled into the yard and clattered to a stop late in the afternoon, Mrs. Albrecht climbed down, hot and dusty but smiling. She handed Vic a small sack. There was a Dixie cup and a wooden spoon inside. "You better eat it right away before it all melts."

The vanilla ice cream and orange sherbet had already melted but they were still cold. Vic tipped the cup and drank it. "Boy, that was good. Thanks a lot." He scraped the inside of the cup with the spoon. "Did you have a good time?"

"Oh, yes. Papa took me to the matinee and we saw Richard Dix in a talking picture." She gave her husband a one-armed squeeze and he grinned self-consciously. "And he didn't have one drink all day, either."

Vic took the tarp off the back of the truck. "Shall I take the groceries in?"

"Yes. I got some things to make a cake with. I'll go start the fire so we can have it for supper."

15

Toward the end of the month Vic began thinking happily about his wages. Twenty dollars, less the cost of the shoes and socks, would leave him almost fifteen. That was a lot of money!

On the first of June, when nothing had been said about paying him, he asked about it.

"I got nothing now," Mr. Albrecht said. "I'll pay you when the cherries get ripe next month."

Vic was disappointed but he told himself that next month he'd have forty dollars coming. It was worth waiting for.

June passed, the days got hotter and dustier and the cherries began to ripen. The first week of July pickers came from neighboring ranches and Mr. Albrecht took a truckload of cherries to Ephrata. He didn't come back for three days, and Mrs. Albrecht cried most of the time. He returned unshaven, smelling of alcohol. Vic asked about his pay.

"Next month," Mr. Albrecht promised. "Next month you'll get what you got coming."

The white mare had been showing signs of nervousness and was becoming difficult to handle. "Better stop working her," Mr. Albrecht advised, so they left her in the corral. But she was still nervy, she paced back and forth, looking out over the sagebrush, nickering and sniffing deeply of the spicy air.

"She would like to have a husband," Mrs. Albrecht said.

A few nights later, Vic was awakened by the crack of breaking wood. Jumping out of bed he ran to the window and looked out. The moon was full and by its light he could see the wild horses milling in the swirling dust, the sweaty animals glistening in the moonlight.

Vic was so stirred by the sight that he did not see a figure break from the shadow of the house or notice Mr. Albrecht hurrying across the farmyard. When he ducked inside and stood at the window, Vic was startled to see a Winchester in his hands.

"You're not going to *shoot* him, are you?" Vic asked.

"Not that fellow," Mr. Albrecht said as the stallion jumped over the broken rails of the corral, snorted and headed for the open country. "He'll give me a good foal. I'm after the others."

As the band followed the stallion, Mr. Albrecht stepped out of the shack, aimed his gun and fired.

A half-grown colt shrieked, its hindquarters buckled, and it went down with a broken back. Another shot and another young horse screamed and went down. Mr. Albrecht fired three more shots in quick succession at the departing band. A horse stumbled, whinnied, but managed to hobble after its companions on three legs. The stallion cut back from the lead and put himself between the other wounded horses and the rifleman.

Mr. Albrecht levered the last empty shell from his 30-30. The colt with the broken back was trying to escape by pulling its dragging hindquarters along with its front feet. The other was floundering in the dust like a beheaded chicken. "What did you do that for?" Vic demanded.

"I can get two cents a pound for horse meat in town." The rancher reloaded, went to each of the crippled animals and shot it between the eyes. Now they were dead, but Vic could still hear their cries above the fading thud of hoofbeats.

"You go to my shed and get a lantern and a couple knives," Mr. Albrecht ordered. "We got to bleed these fellows and butcher them so I can take the meat to town in the morning."

"Count me out, Mr. Albrecht! I won't butcher horses."

"You better, or you pack your stuff and get off my place."

"That suits me fine. How about the money I've got coming?"

"You'll have to wait till I get it."

Vic went into the shack and switched on the light. He dressed hastily in his new clothes, and put his other belongings in a feed sack.

The eastern sky was just beginning to brighten when he came out. Smoke was coming from the chimney of the house; the kitchen light was on and he could see Mrs. Albrecht moving about inside. He put the sack down outside the door and went in.

"My, you look good in your new clothes, Wiktor, but why are you up so early?"

"I came to say good-by, Ma'am. I'm leaving."

"What is the matter?"

"Your husband fired me. I won't help butcher those wild horses he just shot."

"He is a cruel, cruel man."

"Well, thanks for all you've done for me, Mrs. Albrecht—and good-by."

"You can't go without some breakfast. Now, you sit down and I will fix you something." She put on coffee, fried some eggs and made toast on top of the stove.

"You should go home, Wiktor. Your mudder will be lonesome for you." She poured his coffee and served scorched toast and leathery eggs. "How will you get there?"

"I don't know—hitchhike, hop a freight, maybe."

"You better wait and ride to town with Papa. When he sells the horse meat he can pay you what we owe you, then you can ride the passenger train."

Vic shook his head. "I want to get out of here as fast as I can."

Mrs. Albrecht looked at Vic. Then she went into the other room and came back with an old coin purse. She counted a dollar in change. "Here, you can't leave without any money at all. Write your mudder's address for me and I'll send the rest when we sell the fruit this fall."

He wrote down the address and finished his breakfast.

"You got to have some lunch, too," Mrs. Albrecht said. "What would you like?"

"Oh, a few onions and carrots and spuds will be all right."

"That won't make a good lunch."

"It will if I can find a jungle and a boilin'-up can."

She looked puzzled.

"I mean it will make a good stew."

"Oh." She put the vegetables and some bread into a paper bag. "I—I wish you could stay, Wiktor. It has been good to have a happy boy whistling and singing around the place again."

"I—I couldn't." He jerked open the door, picked up his sack of things and threw it over his shoulder.

She reached up and kissed him quickly on the cheek, then put a hand to her eyes and went back inside. Vic turned and hurried down the orchard lane, fighting back a guilty feeling. But nothing on earth could keep him here another day, another hour.

He hadn't been walking an hour when a truck loaded with baled hay came along and picked him up. Just before eight o'clock the driver pulled onto the platform of the scales across the tracks from the depot at Ephrata to weigh his load. Vic got out and asked the scale attendant the best way to get to Wenatchee.

"Some trucker heading west will stop here sooner or later. Stick around."

Sitting in the scale house, Vic told the attendant he'd been working at the Albrecht ranch for the past two months. "Well," the man said, "you sure lasted longer than most of them."

The sound of a whistle came from down the railroad tracks. Vic stepped out of the scale house and watched the train come in. "I think I'll see if I can get out of here on the blinds."

"You'd better watch your step," the scale man said. "Some of those conductors get a big kick out of putting guys off in the middle of the desert."

"Thanks, but I'll give it a try."

At the call of "'Bort!" from the other side of the train, Vic began walking toward the crossing as though on his way to town. The whistle blew, the brakes hissed, and the train began to move. Vic stopped, as if waiting for the cars to clear so he could cross the tracks. As the engine went by he waved to the fireman and got a friendly highball in return. The cab passed and as the tender came along Vic reached for the stirrup at the rear end of it with his foot, caught the grabiron and swung aboard. Nothing to it!

He got up onto the ledge, hopped across the couplers, and stepped back into the vestibule at the front of the baggage coach. He was on his way! He sat down on his sack and relaxed. The conductor had a schedule to keep and if there was any throwing-off to be done, it would probably be at a regular stop and not in the desert—he hoped.

The train pulled into the next station, out again, and Vic felt safer. When they'd gained speed Vic dropped his caution and came out of the vestibule. He stepped across the couplers and rode standing on the ledge, hanging onto the handrail at the rear of the tender.

The land was table-flat and, except for rare stops at far-apart stations, they made good time. Ahead, the mountains were becoming taller and the individual crags and canyons began to show in sharp detail. Vic was hungry. He ate half of his loaf of bread and peeled and ate a raw potato to help quench his thirst.

"Hey, Slim!"

He looked up, startled.

The fireman was standing atop the tender. "The yard bulls will catch you if you ride into the station!" he yelled. "Better hop off when we slow down at Appleyard!"

"Thanks! How did you know I was here?"

The fireman grinned. "I saw you get on at Ephrata."

He went back to the cab and Vic got his sack from the vestibule. He hadn't been so smart after all!

When the train slowed down by the icing sheds, he watched for his chance and dropped off. A jungle filled with hobos was just across the tracks, and they all must have seen him come in on the varnish! He couldn't help but swagger a bit as he approached a group squatted around a fire watching a boilin'-up can. He peered in. The mulligan looked kind of thin. "How about helping out?" he asked.

"Sure, what you got?" the fire-tender asked.

"An onion, couple of carrots."

"Put 'em in."

In an hour the mulligan was ready and Vic sipped his share from an old tomato can. Unsalted and meatless, it tasted watery and wasn't very filling. He was still hungry, but he decided to save the rest of his bread to munch on going over the hump tonight.

"Do you know when the next westbound drag is leaving?" he asked the hobo who had been tending the fire.

"Almost any time now."

Vic picked up his sack. "Anybody else going west?"

No one moved. "Hardly anybody's been goin' west the last few days," a fellow said. "Everybody's headin' this way on account of the forest fires."

"Forest fires?"

"Yeah, I hear they been raidin' the jungles and yankin' guys off the drags to fight fire."

"You mean they're running away from work?"

"Yep."

"I thought everybody was looking for it."

"Nope."

Vic knew he could hold his own with almost anybody on a fire line. But wasn't it kind of early for bad blazes?

The big fires generally didn't break out until later in the month, or August, when the woods got really dry. Lately, though, the radio had been reporting that there hadn't been so little rainfall for many years. He wondered where the fires were—on the Peninsula? Maybe he could help knock down a blaze or two and pick up a few dollars. Then, if he decided to go home, he wouldn't get there broke. He'd have something in his pocket to show for the time he'd been away.

A set of motors came humming along and coupled onto a string of freight cars standing in the yard. "Looks like your rattler is about to leave town, Slim," someone said.

Vic decided to keep traveling.

16

When the train came out of the Cascade Tunnel, a blood red sun above the crags, blue haze hanging in the valleys, and a smoky scent told of the forest fires burning somewhere. It was late in the afternoon when they stopped in the yards at Skykomish. The train crew went to dinner and the hostler replaced the motors with a Malley.

Vic had finished the bread he'd been saving, but was still hungry. He wanted to go buy something solid but was reluctant to spend his dollar, so stayed in the gondola, nibbling on a raw carrot.

When the crew returned and the drag pulled out of Skykomish, the memory of what had happened to Blackie there was so sharp Vic closed his eyes.

Riding along, looking over the side of the gondola, he watched the lights of tiny villages going by. As the sky darkened, the air grew chill and he put on his mackinaw.

At Everett, empties were switched off and men began calling in the darkness, "Up on the tops, boys; up on the tops!"

Vic heard their footfalls in the cinders and some men climbed into the gondola. A whistle, drawbar rattlings, a jerk, and they were on their way again.

They passed docks and boatyards where the tang of salt beach and seaweed was stronger than the smell of burning forests. Vic's mouth watered for a steamed clam or raw oyster.

On around the curve they went, and the lights of Seattle glowed against the smoky sky. At Ballard the train slowed and rumbled over the bridge across the canal, then through the cut, and they stopped between the yard office and the roundhouse. "All out, boys, end of the line!"

Fires were flickering in the jungle, and sleeping men were stretched out on the ground around it. "All right if I warm up a bit?" Vic asked, his teeth chattering.

The old man tending the fire nodded and added a stick of wood. Vic sat down on his bumpy sack and held his hands to the flames. Overhead, he could just make out the moon trying to shine through the haze. "I wonder where those forest fires are?" he commented.

"Half of Oregon is going up in smoke," the old man said.

Oregon! The word set his foot to itching. If the fires

were in Oregon, then why not go on to Oregon? It wasn't really very far away. "Say, Mister, how do you get to Oregon, anyway?"

The old man gestured to the south. "They're makin' up the Portland manifest down in the other end of the yards right now."

Vic left the jungle and cut across the tracks to the cinder path on the other side. He'd gone about half a mile when he saw the red lights on the rear end of a caboose that was coupled to a drag. A kerosene lamp was burning in the caboose and he could see two men inside.

He passed his hand along the side of each boxcar, feeling for an open door. There were none. Ahead, he heard the whistle of an engine, and the brake gear underneath the cars began to creak. If he didn't find an empty soon, it was up on the tops again. And he still didn't know whether this was the train he wanted. He heard voices ahead, then his hand told him he had come to a flatcar. "Is this the Portland manifest?"

"This is it!" someone answered from the darkness.

Vic found the stirrup and a grabiron and climbed on. The rattle of drawbars coming down the train warned him to watch out for a jolt. It came and went, and he was on his way to Oregon.

As daylight outlined the hills, a mist began forming in the lowlands. The sun rose higher and the wind sweeping over the cars became pleasantly warm. The day was going to be a hot one—forest fire weather if he'd ever seen it. Kalama, Woodland, Ridgefield, went by at sixty miles an hour. He was seeing the country now! They slowed at the outskirts of Vancouver, and passing through the yards went by a Missouri Pacific boxcar with "TEX K.T." daubed on it in yellow paint.

They crept across a steel bridge from which he could look into the funnels and open hatches of ocean freighters moored along the Columbia. Tugs and barges and log rafts were moving up and down the river. Halfway across, Vic began to feel excited. He must be in Oregon now! The far shore of the river looked about the same as the side they'd left, but just being in another state for the first time in his life made it feel different, anyway.

On either side of the tracks, idle men sat outside the rickety doors of their shacks. Gaunt, unsmiling women and ragged children picked berries along the embankment. A city appeared on the higher ground ahead, and the train entered a vast railroad yard and stopped.

"Portland!" someone called. "Watch out for the yard bulls here."

Vic made for the tall buildings in the middle of town, looking for a place to eat.

The aroma from the open door of a little lunch room was inviting. He walked in and took a seat at the counter.

The white-capped cook gestured toward the menu

lettered on a card over the stove. "Something for you, Slim?"

"Stack of hotcakes, two eggs, a slice of ham, and coffee, please."

"Got the money to pay for it?"

"Sure." Vic dug out fifty cents and laid it on the counter. The cook put it in the cash register and brought him a cup of coffee. When his breakfast was ready he polished it off and ordered another stack of hotcakes. They cost him fifteen cents more, but he couldn't go looking for a job on an empty stomach.

Vic struck up a conversation with the cook. "Up in Seattle I heard there were a lot of forest fires down here."

"Yep. I guess they're pretty bad."

"Where would I find out about getting a job on the fire line?"

"The Forest Service, I suppose."

A fellow sitting down the counter spoke up. "If you're lookin' for work you've come to the wrong place, stranger. We've got too many of our own people on relief to let outsiders hog the jobs."

Another man said, "Why didn't you stay in Washington? They've got fires there, too."

An hour later Vic was standing in the shade of a drawbridge, looking out across a river, hearing streetcars rumble overhead. It was only midmorning but already the day was a scorcher. He was hot and thirsty, and his new shoes hurt his feet.

The river bank was lined with old industrial buildings, their long unopened doors secured by rusty padlocks. Upstream, where a refuse dump extended into the river, human scavengers had come to search for food.

A thin old man on crutches, knee-deep in refuse, snatched a piece of soggy bread from the pile and popped it into his mouth. Some were after bits of wood and boxes; others salvaged papers and bottles. On the shore side of the dump was a community of shacks.

As he turned in the opposite direction, Vic saw a heavy-set man coming toward him. He carried a mackinaw over one arm and wore a billed cap low on his forehead. Under the other arm he carried a cabbage. He seemed to be scanning the ground before him. As he came near he looked up and grinned. "You wouldn't have any smokin', would you, Slim?"

"No, I don't smoke."

The man wiped sweat from his face with the back of a chubby hand. "It's too hot to be out in the sun. Let's park ourselves in the shade." They sat down in the doorway of one of the vacant buildings. He looked at Vic's shoes. "New shoes, new pants, new shirt—you must've busted into a store."

"No. I still owe for the clothes, and the shoes are all I've got to show for two months' work."

"Well, if you're goin' to be ridin' the rods, you'd better mess up those duds and get your shoes scuffed.

Somebody's liable to think you're prosperous and rap you on the head."

"They wouldn't get much."

"You look like you might have come off a farm."

Vic nodded.

"How'd you get to be a hobo?"

Vic told of being turned down by the Navy and the CCC in Seattle and of going to the waterfront to watch the ship come in. "A rattler came along, I hooked a ride and here I am."

"How do you like bein' a knight of the road?"

"I like traveling and seeing new country all right, but I sure don't like begging and going hungry."

"It takes a little practice." The chubby man peeled two leaves from his cabbage. "Have some salad." He gave Vic one leaf and began to munch the other. "What would you have had for breakfast this morning if you was back home, Slim?"

Vic shrugged.

"Did your folks keep chickens?"

"Uh-huh."

"Then I'll bet there'd have been eggs."

"Yes."

"And with those cows you'd probably have milk and butter?"

"Oh, sure."

"Did your mother ever make biscuits?"

"She makes real good biscuits—and cornbread, too."

"Hot biscuits and butter and fried eggs!"

"And blackberry jam and wild honey, too."

"Wow! You was sittin' right on top of the Big Rock Candy Mountain and didn't even know it. What did you run off and leave all that for?"

Vic looked away and did not reply. But there was something about this man that made it easy to talk to him, and before long he'd told the whole story.

"A guy can take only so much," he ended. "Do you blame me for leaving?"

"Gosh, no! With that stepdad—if he's like you say —you had a lot to put up with. But I never did see a kid that didn't think his folks was givin' him a bad time." The man chuckled, as though that resolved everything.

Nibbling on the cabbage, they watched the river traffic. At the whistle of deep-sea freighters or stern-wheeled river vessels, the drawbridge would swing open and let them through. Men went by in row-boats, fishing; boys on flimsy rafts paddled off on great expeditions.

Vic began thinking of the boat he'd always wanted to build, and how mad he'd been when Mom gave the boards to the Smiths for their new roof. How long ago that seemed. Why, he'd just been a kid then—with no more sense than these kids paddling out on their raft—thinking the adventures they dreamed of were coming true.

After a time Vic's new companion said, "So you like to travel, eh?"

"I guess I've got an itchy foot."

"How'd you like to team up with me for a trip to California?"

California! The very name made Vic tingle. "I've never been there."

"String along with me, Slim, and you'll see a lot of other places, too."

The invitation was tempting. California wasn't too far away, and it would be nice to say he'd been there. That was more than most of the Peninsula boys could boast of. But the mood he'd got in watching the boys on the river had stirred up a great wave of homesickness, greater than any he had felt until now. Fighting it back, he finally said, "I'd like to . . . yes, I'll go."

"Good."

They shook hands on it. "By the way, Slim, everybody calls me Heavy."

17

They spent the remainder of the afternoon sitting in the shade of the warehouse talking. Heavy had served in the Army in the World War. Afterward he'd gone to sea and had the tattoos on his arms and chest to prove it.

"Wish I could have got in the Navy," Vic said.

"You can always try again," Heavy told him, "but right now it's time we went to work." He picked up his coat and cabbage and got to his feet as the five o'clock whistles blew. They walked to a heavily traveled intersection where homebound motorists had to stop for a traffic light. "This is a good stand," he said. "You work the far corner and I'll take care of this one."

"What am I supposed to do?"

"Shoot snipes." The passenger in a car waiting for the light to change flipped a cigarette butt out the window. Heavy retrieved it from the gutter, stubbed it out and dropped it into a tobacco can he carried.

"See, there's nothin' to it." He spotted a couple more and picked them up. "Traffic lights are a gold mine. Lightin' a fresh smoke gives them drivers somethin' to do while they're waitin' for the green."

Vic crossed to the other corner. He saw a butt smoldering on the sidewalk. He hesitated, looking around, then scooped it up, hoping no one had seen him. Shooting snipes was almost as bad as knocking on back doors. But the first one was the hardest; soon it got to be a game, like picking mushrooms, to see how many you could get. He even got to dodging out into the street to nail them before the light turned green and the car wheels squashed them. By the time Heavy signaled to come back he had a handful.

"Say, you did all right," Heavy said when he saw Vic's take. They stepped into a doorway and he pinched the burned end off each butt, split the paper and put the tobacco into his can. "My own private blend." He rolled a cigarette, lighted up and inhaled deeply.

"Can you sing?"

"A little."

"Know any church songs?"

"Sure."

"All right, let's go to dinner, then."

They had walked several blocks down a dingy side street to an old store building. The window frames were painted white and a sign in bright red letters read:

SISTER KATHERINE'S BREAD OF LIFE MISSION

Heavy rolled the cabbage in his mackinaw. "Kate puts out about the best handout on the skid road. When the singin' starts, beller your lungs out. The loudest voices get the most soup."

The service was nearly over when they arrived.

"We're lucky we missed the sermon," Heavy whispered. He led the way down the aisle. Vic followed, but he felt uncomfortable. He was a Methodist and he'd gone to church all his life, but he had never seen a woman preacher before. He followed Heavy as though he were hypnotized.

"And now we will raise our voices in song," Sister Katherine was saying as she went to the organ, sat down and began to pump the pedals. "We will sing 'Beulah Land, Sweet Beulah Land,'" she announced, and swung into the old familiar tune. Heavy joined in, loud and clear. His baritone wasn't bad at all. Then came "Rock of Ages" and other easily remembered hymns that anyone could sing. And singing them made Vic feel good.

Sister Katherine went back to the pulpit and closed the service with prayer, a begging of forgiveness for the sinners of the world. "That's all, boys," she ended abruptly. "Is everybody ready to eat?"

"And how!"

Sister Katherine led the way through a door to a back room where a table and benches were set up and pots were simmering on a gas stove. She put an apron on over her robe and began slicing bread, filling soup bowls and coffee cups. When everyone was served she took a seat at the head of the table, asked a blessing, and they all began to eat. The soup contained mostly rice and potatoes, the bread was dry and stale, the coffee was weak, but altogether it was filling. As each man finished he took his dishes to a sink and washed them. "Bless you, Sister," they said, and left.

Heavy was a slow eater and lingered over his food. After everyone else had gone Sister Katherine filled his and Vic's bowl again. When they'd had enough she said, "You going to try to get work here, boys?"

"No, we're headin' for sunny Cal tonight," Heavy said as he got up from the table. A train whistle sounded in the distance. "That's probably our rattler makin' up now. Thanks for everything, Kate."

Sister Katherine accompanied them to the door. "I'm glad you boys dropped by. Be sure and come in when you hit town again, Heavy. You, too, Slim."

They left the mission and headed toward the river. It was getting dusk and the feeble yellow street lights were coming on. Vic felt uneasy in the skid road district and noticed that Heavy, too, chose to walk out near the curb and not close to the entrances to alleyways. After a time Vic said, "What kind of religion is that, anyway?"

"I don't know what she calls it, Slim, but Kate believes in it and that's what counts."

"Where does the grub come from?"

"She scrubs floors and washes clothes so she can feed hungry people. She's a *real* workin' Christian and not just a talkin' one, and as far as I'm concerned she can dish her religion out any way she likes."

When they got to the dismal warehouse district near the river, where railroad tracks and trolley wires ran down the middle of the street, fifty or so men were sitting on the curbstones. Heavy inquired about the Oregon Electric freight train. "She'll be along pretty soon," he was told. They sat down on the curb to wait.

From up the street they heard the rumble of box-cars. A headlight came around a curve and everybody got up as the freight train came into view. It was just a little branch line rattler, not over twenty cars long, pulled by two small electric locomotives. The crew paid no attention as the hobos began to climb aboard. The railroad police, if any, looked the other way, no doubt thankful that another load of hungry transients was leaving their territory.

There were several empties on the head end but Heavy let them go by. "It's too nice to be cooped up inside tonight." Pressing the cabbage close to his side with his elbow, he caught a grabiron and went to the tops. Vic joined him on the catwalk.

The moon was just rising above the eastern mountains as the train left the city lights behind and went rocking up the riverbank and rattling off across the countryside. The trolley left streaks of sizzling blue flame as it burned away the grime that had accumulated on the overhead wire since a train had last gone this way. The headlight cut a swath down the tree-lined tracks ahead, and the caboose lamps trailed along behind. On either side, near and far away, yellow lights shone from farmhouse windows.

18

Two mornings later, Vic wakened in a boxcar on a sidetrack beside a river. Sunlight streamed through the door and onto the sleeping men sprawled on the floor. He was startled by the sight of two young girls in a corner, just a few feet away. He looked around for Heavy, but he was missing. Already up and off to the jungle, most likely.

Vic jumped out to look for him. The jungle was in a woodsy spot between tracks and riverbank, and as he expected, Heavy was there, smoking a cigarette and tending a sooty gunboat over a fire.

"Say, there's a couple of girls in that car, Heavy."

"That's why I got out."

"Where did they get on?"

"Darned if I know. They were there when I woke up."

"They're not bad looking."

"Stay away from 'em," Heavy warned as he took from his pocket a sock, filled with coffee grounds Vic had scrounged the day before. He put it in the gunboat and chunked it up and down.

"Where are we, anyway?" Vic asked.

"Grants Pass, Oregon."

"How far is it to California?"

"About a hundred miles."

"I wonder how long we'll be here?"

"This is Saturday and nothin' moves till Monday. It'll give us a chance to get cleaned up."

They went to the river, washed their clothes and hung them up on bushes. They bathed and had a swim, then sat enjoying the sun.

When their clothes were dry and they had dressed, they followed the railroad tracks to town. In a small park near the depot, they found a public rest room and Heavy shaved. Vic looked in the mirror and examined the few silky wisps sprouting from his own chin. "I suppose I ought to shave, too."

"If you put cream on 'em, a cat could lick 'em off," Heavy said.

They went out to the residential district where Vic mowed lawns, split wood and washed cars in return for handouts. Heavy waited discreetly in the background and took charge of the loot as Vic returned from each foray.

They went back to the park at noon and sat down on an unoccupied spot under a tree. The park was filled with families eating basket lunches or taking their ease in the shade. It was the same kind of crowd that might be seen in any small town on a summer afternoon, country people in for the week's shopping. Children ran and scuffled, boys played catch, old ladies fanned themselves, men talked about the crops.

A pretty girl in a yellow dress looked toward Vic over her parents' shoulders. Their eyes met and both looked away quickly. He had never paid much attention to girls; he'd rather have a good dog around. But he couldn't keep his eyes off this tall, slender girl. Her eyes were blue and she had brown hair that glistened in the specks of sunlight that slanted through the foliage overhead. He heard her mother call her Jean.

Vic wished he had the nerve to say something to her. But no decent girl would speak to a stranger, and especially a hobo. It was an exciting experience, the occasional meeting of their eyes. It was disturbing, too. He'd never felt this way before.

Late in the afternoon a cooling wind sprang up and the people began leaving the park. Regretfully, Vic watched the girl go, carrying a lunch basket in one hand, leading a younger sister with the other. She glanced back, then was lost in the crowd.

Vic and Heavy went out and worked the town again.

The sun went down behind the hills across the river and with the coming dusk the lights came on. A policeman noticed them and said, "I think you fellows better go back to the jungle now. We'd just as soon not have transients around town after dark."

"Thanks for telling us, Officer," Heavy said. "By the way, where's the Catholic church?"

The policeman pointed. "Down that way. You can't miss it."

"Would you object if I went to Confession first?"

"No, and I'm sure the father would be glad to have you come."

"I think I'll do that, then."

"But you go straight to the jungle when you leave the church."

"I certainly will, Officer, I certainly will."

The policeman left.

"Want to go to Confession, Slim?"

"I'm not a Catholic."

"Neither am I, but a priest is always good for a touch." He picked up his mackinaw. He gave the cabbage to Vic and said. "You go back to the jungle and I'll be along later. See if you can get in on a mulligan." He walked off toward the church and Vic picked up his balloon and went to the jungle.

He could hear the laughter of men moving around in the light of a big fire. Someone began to play a violin, another a guitar, and then there was singing. "What's going on down there?" Vic asked.

An old man took off his glasses, squinted his eyes and cupped a hand to an ear. "I'd say they were having a dance."

Vic stood up to see better. Sure enough, two young fellows and a couple of girls in overalls were dancing. The music was crude but it was fast and lively. Vic's foot began to tap. Someone was thumping out the rhythm on a can. The music stopped and everyone yelled, "Wahoo!"

"Why don't you go join 'em, son?" the old man suggested.

"Well, I don't know . . ."

"Oh, go enjoy yourself. You're only young once."

"I guess I will."

Reaching the circle of the fire he found a place near the musicians. The fiddler didn't hold his instrument under his chin but sawed away at it in his lap. The guitarist appeared to be a Mexican. A lean Negro was beating on the bottom of a boilin'-up can. They were playing "She'll Be Comin' 'Round the Mountain." Vic took out his mouth organ and joined in. A dozen hobos were doing a square dance with the two girls whom he'd seen asleep in the boxcar. The fiddler was calling. "Change partners!" The girls kept changing off with the men, and men were dancing with each other. The music stopped. "Wahoo!"

The drummer grinned. "You're doin' all right, Slim!"

Somebody brought a gunboat. Each of the musicians took a drink from it, made a face and passed it on. It came to Vic. "What is it?"

"Gasoline and buttermilk!"

It looked like buttermilk and smelled like gasoline. "No, thanks!"

Every dance was a tag dance. They played "Shine On, Harvest Moon" and the girls waltzed around the rough and dusty ground with ever changing partners. The orchestra played fox trots, hillbilly tunes, and Dixieland jazz. Between numbers the gunboat was passed around. It was shoved at Vic again. "Don't be a piker, Slim! It'll make you forget your troubles!"

"I don't want to blow up."

They played another waltz, "When the Blue of the Night Meets the Gold of the Day." One of the young girls and a young hobo were dancing close together in the shadows away from the fire. An older man tried to cut in and was pushed away. He grabbed the girl by the arm, jerked the two apart.

"You don't push me, you!" The young hobo hit him in the nose and knocked him down. He jumped up, blood streaming.

"Why, you!" A hand darted to a pocket, a knife came out, and a blade snapped open. The hobo grabbed a stick of firewood, brought it down on the older man's head. He fell to his knees. The girls screamed.

"Break it up!"

"Naw, let 'em go!"

The young hobo screamed. "I'm gonna boot your brains out, you——!"

Someone grabbed him. "Take it easy, Lefty!"

"You're askin' for big trouble, Lefty!"

Someone grabbed the peacemaker, another grabbed the grabber; in an instant everybody was involved.

Vic tried to back out of the way of a pair of fellows slugging it out. He stepped on a foot and someone hit him. He hit the fellow back. Someone else hit him. The drummer was bouncing his boilin'-up can off every head that came within reach and producing satisfying thumps. Vic swung at everyone who swung at him until a powerful hand got hold of his collar and jerked him into the shadows. He tried to break free. "Let loose of me!"

It was Heavy. He released his hold. "What's got into you anyway, Slim? You been drinkin' some of that poison?"

"No."

"I catch you in a deal like that again and you're on your own."

Vic's hands were shaking with excitement. "I just went over to watch them dance and I was playing my mouth organ and a couple of them got into an argument about one of the girls and then everybody went at it."

"Are you hurt?" Heavy asked.

Vic flexed his hands. "Just a couple bruised knuckles is all."

"You're lucky."

They spent the night in the jungle and were awakened early the next morning by church bells ringing.

"What say we go to church, Slim?" Heavy said. "What's your religion?"

"Methodist. What's yours?"

"Taking care of *me* is *my* religion. Come on, let's go to your church."

They went to the park and cleaned up, then found a Methodist church. They sang the hymns loud and clear and listened to the sermon attentively. The theme was the prodigal son.

Heavy timed their departure so as to be the last to leave when the services were finished. Stopping at the door to shake hands with the minister, he said, "You certainly inspired me, Reverend."

"Thank you, and may I congratulate you two on your voices. I'd like to have you in my choir."

"Well thanks, I'd like to, Reverend, but we're just in town for the weekend. There's work for us in California."

"Well then, at least let me . . ." The minister reached in his pocket and pulled out a dollar bill.

19

There couldn't be a better place from which to see the world than the catwalk of a boxcar. Even Pullman travelers didn't have a view like this of the hills of southern Oregon. So thought Vic Martin as the Southern Pacific freight train wound up the valley of the Rogue on Monday morning. He could see the old gold diggings on the slopes and modern-day placer miners panning for nuggets the Stampeders might have missed. It was a good day to be traveling, and he was glad to be on the move again.

And now, with every click of the wheels, they were getting nearer California. The sky was blue, the air was clear, and a range of mountains was ahead. At Ashland they stopped to change engines and crews. The train was met by a policeman and a man wearing a Salvation Army cap.

"You'll be here for about an hour," the policeman said. "If you want a meal, go with the captain and you'll be fed. But if I find anybody working the back doors, you'll get thirty days at hard labor. Is that fair enough?"

"Fair enough, Chief."

The Salvation Army man led them up the street to a building with the red shield over the door. Each man was asked his name as he entered, and his home town and occupation were written in a register. "What name did you give 'em, Slim?" Heavy asked.

"My own. Why?"

Heavy shook his head. "Never use your own monicker. Some day you might not want anybody to know you was a hobo or where all you been, so it's best to keep your tracks covered."

There were benches and tables inside. Every man was given a big bowl of pinto beans with salt pork, a generous slab of cornbread, and a cup of coffee.

As they ate, the sounds of a small brass band practicing familiar hymns came from a room above them: "Rock of Ages," "The Old Rugged Cross," and "Onward Christian Soldiers."

During the meal a lady in a Salvation Army lassie's bonnet and uniform announced that clothing was available in the next room for anyone who needed it. "Let's go see if we can find a shirt my size," Heavy said when they had finished eating.

In the other room, men were trying on second-hand shoes and used garments. While Heavy was looking for a shirt to fit him, an old man came in and spoke to the lady in attendance. "Say, Sister, you got any teeth that might fit me?"

She took down a shoe box from a shelf. It was filled with old dental plates. She took out a set. "Try these." He put them in his mouth, tried to chew. "The uppers are pretty good but the lowers are too wide in back."

"Let's try another, then." He handed back the plate and she sorted through the box. "Here, see how this fits." He put it in.

Vic turned away. "I'll see you outside, Heavy."

Soon after Vic and Heavy returned to the train and got into a boxcar, a thin, poorly dressed young couple came down the path beside the track. The boy carried a battered suitcase and a roped-up bundle of tattered patchwork quilts. The girl pushed a decrepit baby carriage. Stopping by the boxcar door, the young man asked, "You got room in there for the wife and kids and me?"

"Sure," Heavy said. "Come right in."

The bedding and suitcase were handed up and the carriage, with a wide-eyed toddler and a sleeping baby in it, was boosted in. The husband helped his wife up, then clambered in himself.

Heavy went to one end of the car. "All right, boys, what do you say we let these kids have this end to themselves?" Everyone cleared out except a dirty, unshaven tramp. "All right, fella, let's move."

"I ain't movin' for nobody."

Heavy caught the tramp by the collar, jerked him to his feet, belly-bumped him half the length of the boxcar, then belly-bumped him out the door.

They left Ashland with two engines on the head end and a helper pushing. The route was one of winding turns, tall bridges over chasms, black and smoky tunnels. The slopes were steep, the forests dense, the view spectacular. Late in the afternoon they left the helper at the summit and began braking down the other side. Just before sunset they passed a sign, "Orcal," and Heavy said, "This is California, Slim. What do you think of it?"

"It looks just like Oregon." The thrill of entering another state was absent.

Some time in the night the train came to a jarring stop. Rain was beating on the boxcar roof and lights were shining through the doors. Vic could hear engines moving down the tracks outside, and the men muttering in the darkness. Someone went to the door and announced the station: "Dunsmuir."

In the head end of the car the children began to fret and the toddler's cry became more and more insistent and irritating. Heavy got up, struck a match and lighted his way to where the little family was settled. "That kid's hungry, son."

"I know, Mister, but we haven't got anything to feed him. And we won't have till we get to my folks' place in Sacramento."

"That won't be till tomorrow night," Heavy said. He came back to Vic. "Slim, are you awake?"

"Yeah. What do you want?"

"Nothing. I'm just going to take a little walk."

Vic watched him get out of the boxcar, cross the tracks, and go up a wet stairway to a town built on a steep hillside.

Less than twenty minutes had passed when Vic heard Heavy come back in. "Get your jackknife out and open one of these cans, Slim."

Vic punched two holes in one can. It was condensed milk. The match Heavy had struck burned out and he lighted another. Vic handed the can to the father; the wailing stopped and the child began to gulp.

"Gee, Mister, I don't know how we'll ever . . ."

"Skip it," Heavy said as he put down three more cans of milk. "This should keep you till you get to Sacramento."

The coupling-on of an engine jarred them. "C'mon, Slim, let's get back where we belong." Heavy struck another match, they found their places and stretched out on the floor again.

"Say, Heavy, where did you get the groceries?" Vic asked.

Heavy did not reply.

When daylight came the rain had stopped, and the boxcar soon was like an oven. It was only a little after nine, but the sun was already high when they stopped in Gerber, a division point deep in the Central Valley.

A one-legged man on crutches came hobbling along the tracks. "Come down off those tops, boys!" he called. "All off for the Jungle Café!" The man moved down the train. "Come down off those tops, boys! Bread and beans and coffee and a place to wash up at the Jungle Café."

"Got any drinking water over there, Stubby?"

"All you want and it's free. Free water at the Jungle Café, boys!" He went on. "Come down off those tops!"

"Let's give it a whirl, Slim." Vic and Heavy got off and followed their guide across a field to an old barn in a grove of oaks. A sign, roughly lettered in white-wash on the side of the barn, read, "JUNGLE CAFE." They had to wait their turn at the water faucet. Some of the fellows only washed and had a drink, then they lay down in the shade of the trees. A number of them, though, lined up to buy a meal.

"You wouldn't think there was so much money in this crowd, would you?" Heavy commented. They washed and drank and got in line.

A rusty cookstove and rows of tables and benches were set up in the barn. The stove was filled with big, steaming pots, tended by a Mexican woman. Her small, pigtailed daughter was washing dishes in a wooden tub. An older woman was collecting the money and serving.

"What's the tariff, Mother?" Heavy asked.

"Hunk of bread and a cup of coffee's a nickel, big bowl of beans for a dime."

Heavy produced a quarter and a nickel. "Beans and bread and coffee for two of us."

234

The bowls were chipped and the cups were cracked, but they were filled. The bread was dry but the chunks were big. Heavy and Vic sat down at a table and had begun to eat when the one-legged man came in.

"Take your time, boys, your train won't be leaving for a while." His eyes missed nothing. "You over there, how about more beans? Only a nickel for a refill." Or, "All right, Shorty, cough up that spoon I saw you put in your pocket." He stood at the exit and checked to see that no one walked off with any utensils. When Vic and Heavy got up to leave he said, "Say, you two look like you could handle a refill. Only cost you a nickel apiece."

"You don't serve beans the way I like 'em," Heavy said.

"You tell me how you like 'em, and we'll serve 'em."

"I like 'em free."

"That's the one way we *don't* serve 'em, you scoundrel."

They found a spot under a tree and stretched out. "That boxcar is sure going to be hot this afternoon," Vic said.

"Yeah. Maybe we'd better take to the tops the rest of the way to Roseville. There won't be any shade up there but at least we'll have some wind."

An engine whistled on the main line. The one-legged proprietor of the Jungle Café came out and looked at his pocket watch. "All aboard, boys! Train now leaving for Roseville with connections for Sacramento,

San Francisco, L.A., Reno, Salt Lake, Denver, and points East! 'Bort!"

The southbound freight was already rolling when Vic and Heavy caught a grabiron and started up.

Beside a stream in the Roseville jungle, Heavy took out the cabbage, no bigger now than a tennis ball. Vic started to sit down. "You better get spruced up and go see what you can hustle, Slim."

While Vic was washing in the stream, Heavy sprawled in the shade on the bank. "I think we'll hit the highway for a change. There's too much competition near the rails."

Vic went on washing in silence.

Heavy took out his tobacco and rolled a cigarette. Looking into the can he said, "By the way, Slim, when you're uptown, keep an eye peeled for snipes. I'm gettin' low on smokin'."

Vic worked the town for two hours and didn't get a handout. On his way through the business district he glanced down an alley and saw an elderly man in a white cook's cap and soiled apron struggling with some heavy garbage cans behind a restaurant. He offered to help and was given a sack of stale pastries in return.

"That's the best I could do, Heavy," he said when he got back to the jungle. "Pickin's are really slim in this burg."

"Did you pick up any smokin'?"

"There's too many other guys been working the main stem."

At nightfall the jungle began filling up. Three young men clad in denims and sombreros, wearing high-heeled boots and carrying saddles, came and settled down nearby. From their conversation Vic gathered they were rodeo riders, en route from one stampede to another.

In the light of a campfire, an agitator stood shaking his fist, trying to organize a bonus march on Washington. "And if they don't give it to us this time we'll take the White House apart!"

An evangelist wandered through, strumming a guitar, singing hymns and preaching the Gospel.

Later, an old man with a scraggly white mustache came carrying a battered violin case in one hand, a sooty gunboat in the other. "Gentlemen," he announced, "I will appreciate any donations you may care to offer." He sat down on a chunk of wood, placed the gunboat before him and took out his violin. He began to saw out and sing some of the sad old ballads Vic's mother used to play on the phonograph at home. "Little Rosewood Coffin," "The Baggage Coach Ahead," "The Dying Cowboy."

Vic turned to Heavy. "Tear-jerker, huh?"

"Ye-ah. Hobos always like these kind of songs—and so do I."

Secretly, Vic liked them, too, but wouldn't have admitted it aloud.

Now and then someone put a potato, a carrot or something else into the old man's gunboat.

"Do you know 'The Black Sheep,' Pop?"

He nodded. An engine whistled down in the yards. When it was silent he began to play and sing the song:

Don't be angry with me, Dad, or drive me from your door.

*I know that I've been wayward, but I won't be anymore—*The approaching engine whistled again, drowning out a line.

You'll find the black sheep loves his dad, far better than the rest.

Vic looked toward the oncoming train, a northbound drag.

As the old man began to play a request for "Where is my Wandering Boy Tonight?" Vic stood up, a confused look on his face.

"What's the matter?" Heavy asked. "You feeling all right?"

Vic turned away abruptly from the fire and headed toward the tracks.

"Vic—wait!" Heavy caught up with him and clamped a hand on his shoulder.

Vic wheeled to face him. "Heavy—I've been thinking . . . I want to go home—and I'm going to catch this drag."

Oddly enough, Heavy didn't seem surprised. He raised a hand in farewell. "So long, Slim. Take care of yourself."

"So long, Heavy." Vic walked quickly to the tracks and swung aboard.

The train went only to Marysville, another depression-hit little California town, and Vic had to wait over until the next afternoon. With time on his hands, he washed his clothes and bathed in a stream. In town he had better luck than in Roseville, and returned to the jungle with half a shopping bag filled with traveling chuck.

The sun was high and hot. Looking for a place to rest, he passed two men sitting in the shade of a pile of ties, and he knew instinctively that Heavy would have classified these two as bums. One spoke as Vic went by. "What's your hurry, Kid?" His voice was thick and raspy.

"I want to get out of this sun."

"There's plenty of room here. We're not proud."

Since there was no other shelter near, he sat down.

"Whatcha got in the sack, Kid?"

"Just some stuff."

"Kind of young to be ridin' the rods, ain't you?"

"Oh, I know my way around."

"Maybe you do and maybe you don't. You need a couple of good partners to show you the ropes."

"Yeah," the other fellow said, scratching vigorously, "you team up with us and we'll make a first-class bo out of you."

"No, thanks. I'm a loner."

Vic didn't like the way the pair kept looking at him

and his shoes, and he didn't like the way they smelled. He got up.

"You're not leavin', are you?"

Vic pointed across the jungle. "I see a guy over there I think I know."

"Stick around, Kid. We just might be able to make you an interestin' proposition."

Without replying, Vic walked off to join a group in the shade of a sidetracked boxcar.

Shortly afterward, a big road engine came up the main line, pulling a string of cars. Vic crossed the tracks, stepped close to the accelerating train, caught a grabiron on a gondola, went up and over the side. Looking out, he saw the two bums sprint across the tracks, catch onto a boxcar and swing aboard. Why did they have to be getting on *this* train? He would have unloaded, but the drag was going fast and the yard was too full of switches to risk it. He kept an eye on the two for a time, but they didn't seem to be at all interested in him, just sat on the tops and watched the scenery going by.

As the afternoon advanced it got too hot for him in the open gondola. He climbed out and up onto the tops, swung over the edge of the roof of an empty boxcar, dropped down inside. He ate a sandwich, then stretched out on the floorboards for a nap.

Something solid landing on the boxcar floor awakened him. Opening his eyes he saw a figure silhouetted against the open doorway. Moments later a second man dropped down from above. "Hello,

Slim. We thought you might like a little company."

Vic got to his feet and reached for his shopping bag. His back was to the rear of the car. The two stood facing him.

With one in front of each doorway, Vic felt like a mouse with two hungry alley cats guarding its exit holes. They had him cornered.

One took a step toward him. "You wouldn't happen to have sanriches in that sack, would you, Slim?"

"I might and I might not."

The other took a forward step. "Maybe you'd better let us have a look."

Vic clutched the handles of the bag. They were edging closer. Whichever way he moved, one was there to block his way. "This is my traveling chuck."

"We're travelin' with you. You ain't gonna be stingy, are you?"

"You'll have to take it away from me."

"And we're just the lads that kin do it, too." They moved in on him.

Vic flung the shopping bag over their heads and out the door. "Help yourself!"

The taller one jabbed a hand into his pocket, pulled out a switchblade knife, popped the long, thin stiletto blade open. The other one took out a blackjack, shook it menacingly. "Now, you just sit down and take them shoes off!"

Their eyes told Vic they were playing for keeps. He looked out at the rough countryside flashing by. He might survive a headfirst plunge through the doorway, but if these two ever got their hands on him, he'd never leave the car alive. "O.K.," he said. "You can have the shoes." He knelt on one knee, fumbled with a lace.

"You're a smart kid. It's simpler for you to take 'em off than for us to have to do it."

His hands were shaking. "I . . . I can't get this knot untied."

"Take your time. You ain't goin' no place. And when you get the shoes off, you better take off your clothes while you're at it."

Down on one knee, in the position of a foot racer, Vic took a chance. He dashed straight at the left-hand doorway. The knife-wielder slashed at him and he felt a stinging pain across his shoulder. The one with the blackjack beat him to the doorway and swung the loaded sap. Vic ducked and the slasher, stepping in close for a stab at his back, caught the blow between the eyes, went down in a heap. The sapper stood open-mouthed, looking down at his buddy. Vic jumped up, caught the door track overhead, put a foot on the latch, scrambled up onto the roof.

He ran down the catwalk, broad-jumped the coupling space, ran another car-length, scuttled down the grabirons to the stirrup. A town was coming up fast. He saw the depot. Most small stations had sand at either end of the platform for the dumping off of mail and freight.

He put a foot out, let loose and went tumbling end-over-end. He stopped rolling and sat up as the car with the tramps in it went by.

He was just getting to his feet when the depot door opened and the station agent came running out. "You could have killed yourself jumping off like that!"

Vic put a hand to his shoulder. It came away bloody. "I had to. A couple of bums just tried to knife me."

The agent looked at his wound and whistled. "You had a close one. They find the bodies of fellows like you along this track every once in a while."

The agent turned toward the depot. "There isn't a doctor around here, but I think my wife can take care of you all right. Come in and take off your shirt."

They bathed his cut and stopped the bleeding. "It's not too deep," the woman said, "but you'll carry the scar to your grave, son." She put iodine on the wound and bandaged it. Then she made some sandwiches and poured a glass of cold buttermilk for him. While he ate, she washed his shirt and hung it in the sun to dry.

"There won't be another train through here until this evening," the station agent said. "Would you like to have supper with us while you're waiting?"

"I sure would."

During the meal they asked about his family and where he was from. He told them.

"We've always wanted to visit the Northwest," the agent said. "What's it like up there?"

"Oh, it's not a bit like it is here in California. Every place you look we've got trees and mountains."

"Are yours any prettier than our Sierras out there?" The man indicated a distant range through the kitchen window.

"Oh, your mountains are pretty all right, but the Olympics are different. They're more jagged and they've always got snow on them." Vic waved a hand in the general direction of the red hills beyond the railroad tracks. "I don't think I could ever get used to open country like this where there aren't any trees. There's woods all around our place," he continued, his face lighting up. "And they're full of rabbits and grouse and deer. An old logging road goes past our barn that takes you to the top of a bluff where you can stand and watch the ships go by."

"Sounds nice," the agent said. "I suppose you're on your way going back there now?"

"Yes—I am. But I kind of dread getting there—"

Vic broke off uncertainly. The agent looked interested so in a moment he blurted out the whole story.

The station agent sat drumming his fingers on the tablecloth. After some moments he said, "We've had a lot of boys stop off here with us and you know it's a funny thing how many of them have stories just like yours. They all think things would be different if they could just change their father's attitude toward them."

"I don't waste any of *my* time thinking that," Vic said. "I'll never be able to change mine."

You can't *expect* to change anyone else," the agent said quickly. "But you can change yourself."

Before Vic could think of a reply, the telegraph instrument clicked in the depot office and the agent went to answer it.

Later, as Vic was about to climb aboard a boxcar, the agent came out to tell him good-by. "God has plans for you, son, or He would never have saved your life today. Never forget that," he said.

20

It was early morning when Vic Martin unloaded from a boxcar at Interbay. He struck off on foot and four hours later was in Edmonds. A covered truck was waiting on the ferry dock. He slipped into the back end of it and when the truck was aboard the boat, he came out of hiding. There was a driver going to Port Angeles, and he said sure Vic could go along. An hour after docking at Port Ludlow Vic hopped out at the county road.

It was a beautiful day. The sky was clear and blue, the air pleasantly warm and sweet. A mile away at the end of the road he could see the house, the barn, and the chickenhouse.

Ripe blackberries hung from the vines that climbed the nearby fence. He stopped and ate a few. Not so much because of hunger, but to savor the taste of them. It was the taste of coming home.

He went on down in the hollow and up over the hump, and as he came over the last rise he stopped.

There it was, the old stump ranch! There was Mom, bent over the tubs, hands moving back and forth on the washboard.

Nancy, in her straw hat, was in the garden picking peas. The pump was creaking and Fred's shoulders rose and fell as he filled a water bucket at the well. The old truck was in the barn and Dad had his head under the hood, tinkering with the engine.

From the chickenhouse a hen cackled, and Struttin' Sam flew up onto a stump, flapped his wings and crowed proudly as though it were *he* who had just laid the egg. Over in the field below the house the cows were grazing, switching their tails to keep away the flies. Vic counted them. There were two new calves.

And down by the gate, that patch of yellow fur lying in the road would be Jack. Vic whistled. The dog stirred, pointed ears came erect. He whistled again and Jack came racing toward him. Vic was down on his knees waiting with outstretched arms. He caught the dog and hugged him.

Vic stood up and Jack went running around and around in circles, yipping in excitement. Nancy looked toward the sound. Then she dropped her basket and came running barefoot across the field toward him.

"Mom! Dad! Freddy! Vic's home!"

AFTERWORD

There is little fiction in this story. It is based
entirely on experiences of my own or of other
boys I met while roaming the West as a teen-
age hobo in the early Thirties. We travelers
in those Depression days were all part of it
and saw it at its worst, and sometimes at
its best. There were rogues and rascals and
brutes among us. But there were others, too.
Of these I like to think that a little of each
rubbed off on me in passing. Had it not, I
might have never been anything but just another "bindle stiff"—a hobo with a "balloon."

Tom E. Clarke

GLOSSARY OF HOBO SLANG
AND EXPRESSIONS

Balloon—Hobo's pack.
Beanery—Railroad eating house.
Big Rock Candy Mountain—Hobo's paradise.
Bindle—A balloon, hobo's pack.
Bindle stiff—Hobo with a balloon.
Blinds—The fore end of a baggage car next to the loco-
motive.
Boilin'-up can—Five-gallon gasoline tin, fitted with wire
handle, used for cooking, washing clothes, bathing,
carrying water, etc.
Brakie—Brakeman.
Brass-pounder—Railroad telegrapher.
Bull—Railroad detective.
Crummy—Caboose, crew's living car at end of freight
train.
—To be infested with lice.
Dingbat—Low class of tramp, a bum.
Drag—Freight train.
Drinkin' can—Small soup can, fitted with wire handle,
used as a cup.

Eatin' can—Tomato can, used for eating, drinking, shaving, etc.

Gon—Gondola car.

Good pickin's—Plentiful handouts.

Gunboat—A gallon can.

Handout—Food begged at back doors.

Highball—A signal.

Hit the back doors—Go begging food.

Hooverville—A semipermanent shacktown.

Jungle—Hobo camp.

Malley—Heavy duty, compound steam locomotive. Also spelled "Mallet."

Manifest—Fast freight train.

Panhandle—To beg money on the streets.

Rattler—Freight train.

Reefer—Refrigerator car.

Ride the rods—Ride a freight train.

Ride the varnish—Ride a passenger train.

Side-door Pullman—Boxcar.

Snake—Switchman.

Snipe—Discarded cigarette butt.

The tops—Tops of boxcars.

Varnish—Passenger train.

Yard—Railroad terminal.